THIS
STONY
GROUND

By the same author . . . .

CALL OF THE HIGH ROAD

THIS STONY GROUND

by

VERA MINSHALL

ZONDERVAN PUBLISHING HOUSE

GRAND RAPIDS - - - - MICHIGAN

Some fell upon stony places, which had not much earth. . . .

Matthew 13:5

CHAPTER ONE

The Rev. Stephen Thornton leaned forward as the car climbed the steep grade. Soon they would be at the top of the hill above Redford, and he would see the old town again.

"Are you so eager to take up your charge?" the Rev. Andrew Gardener, the middle-aged minister who was driving him, remarked smilingly.

"It's my first, remember," Stephen responded, "and packed full of challenges!"

"Yes! You can say that again," was the rejoinder.

As the road leveled out, Stephen silently studied the familiar scene. The hills sloping steeply down to the uneven streets of the small northern town, the stone houses, the wooded valley, the river and the black fingers of the mill chimneys were all a part of his earliest memories. He had loved the rugged grimness of this place, and now he was coming back to the Chapel on Blakelock Hill above High Street, where his grandfather had given so many years of service.

It was a challenge to follow in the footsteps of James Thornton, his grandfather. He had been a great preacher, and his ministry had been blessed with a revival which had made a great impact upon Redford. Adding to the challenge was the fact that Stephen's father had left Redford in disgrace eight years ago!

John Thornton had lacked the Christian faith and the strength of character which his father had. But his honesty had never been questioned until the day when he had been caught stealing money from the safe at the Albion Mill where he was employed.

Everyone's sympathy had gone out to John's shocked wife, his bewildered seventeen-year-old son, and to his father. It seemed such a poor return for the good example he had set. It was chiefly for his family's sake that the firm had taken no action beyond dismissing John Thornton. With his wife and son he then left the district.

James Thornton had carried on in his ministry, almost thankful that his wife had died two years earlier, and had been spared the grief and disappointment which his son had brought upon the family.

Although the minister's faith and enthusiasm remained intact, the numbers attending his services had dwindled until only a small nucleus was left. His challenging sermons did not touch them in their complacency. Old James Thornton died a heart broken man. There had been other ministers, but none of them had stayed long. And now Stephen was on his way to take over Blakelock Hill Chapel. He thought of the difficult years since the family had left Redford. His mother had died soon after, comforted by her son's intention of becoming a minister. To help with finances, Stephen had taken a job and after his father's death had begun his training.

When he had first applied for the charge of the Chapel in Redford, his superiors had questioned the wisdom of his decision.

"Why do you want to go back?" Rev. Gardener had asked, "to prove to the townsfolk that you've made good in spite of your father, or to try to pick up the threads of your grandfather's work?"

"Neither," Stephen had affirmed. "I feel it's God's will. I fought against it for a time, but—I haven't been able to get away from it."

So he had been sent to preach trial sermons at Blakelock Hill, and the people had received him well, as if pleased to discover that he was following in his grandfather's footsteps. Subsequently he had been appointed, and this evening Rev. Gardener was going to officiate at his installation service.

As they drove down the hill towards the Chapel, Stephen remembered his companion's warning: "This is stony ground, you know. It has broken older and more experienced men."

The words echoed in his mind with a sense of foreboding as they approached the home of Mr. and Mrs. William Ogden, with whom Stephen was to lodge.

Stephen climbed out of the car and followed Andrew Gardener through the iron gate and up the flagged path.

Their arrival had evidently been anticipated. Before they reached the front door, it was flung open and the Ogdens greeted

8

them. They were an elderly couple who remembered Stephen from his earliest years.

"Come to the fire," Anne Ogden invited. "The kettle's just boiled. You must be ready for a hot drink."

While they drank cups of hot strong tea, Mrs. Ogden studied the young minister. He was a real 'chip off the old block' she reflected, meaning, of course, his grandfather. Like most other folk in Redford, Anne Ogden preferred to forget John Thornton. She resolved to make Stephen feel at home.

Stephen was a bigger, tougher looking man than his father had been. He had his grandfather's dark, clearly defined brows, grey eyes, and the same strong lines of jaw and chin.

"There'll be a grand crowd tonight!" William stated later over their meal.

Stephen realized that the local folk would be anxious to see how John Thornton's son had 'turned out'. He hoped to rid himself of the 'family label' in time, and get them to accept him on his own merits.

Half an hour before the service was to start the two ministers made their way across to the Chapel. The building was plain almost to the point of ugliness, and felt cold. Its cream colored walls needed painting. But someone had arranged vases of daffodils on the window ledges, and Stephen was grateful for this token of welcome.

In the small vestry the two men knelt to pray for the service ahead, and for Stephen's ministry in the town. As he thought of the challenge facing him, Stephen dedicated himself anew to the work. The earnest longing of his heart resolved itself into a prayer. "Lord, give me revival in this place: revival like that in my grandfather's day. Revival—at all cost!"

Just before the service was due to begin, William Ogden, a deacon, came to the vestry door announcing that the other two deacons wanted to speak to Stephen.

He stepped aside to allow the two men behind him to enter. Stephen remembered them both:—quiet spoken, diplomatic Hubert Craig, and brusque, business-like Henry Bellamy. Hubert managed the large general store on High Street, which had been in the family for generations. His mild blue eyes were welcoming as he took the minister's outstretched hand.

Henry Bellamy was a big, powerful man, with iron grey hair and heavy brows over steel grey eyes. He also came from an old local family. He had climbed from a routine job at the Albion Mill to the position of manager. A local councilman, he was an influential man in the town. There was no hint of warmth in his welcome, however, and Stephen sensed that here was someone who had bitterly resented his appointment.

After exchanging a few conventional words they all went into the Chapel. The building was almost full and Stephen guessed that it was some time since it had housed such a crowd.

Halfway through the singing of the first hymn, a tall dark girl entered. She stood looking around for an empty seat, obviously ill at ease, until one of the ushers took her to a pew near the front.

The simple service began. Stephen was aware that the people were holding themselves in reserve, wondering what to expect from him. He became aware of the restlessness of the girl who had come in late. She did not seem interested in the proceedings, but kept glancing round as though looking for someone. At last the brief addresses of welcome had been given and Stephen's message was over. Everyone crowded through into the schoolroom where refreshments were being served.

Stephen knew that this Saturday evening social had been planned to give him the opportunity of getting re-acquainted with these people on an informal basis. Many of the older folk came up to him, speaking reminiscently of his grandfather. Then an attractive middle-aged woman swept towards him, accompanied by a pretty fair-haired girl.

"It's nice to have you back in Redford, Stephen, or I suppose I should call you Mr. Thornton now," she greeted him warmly. "Wendy has been looking forward to meeting you again."

The girl's blue eyes were shining as Stephen took her outstretched hand. "Wendy Craig!" he exclaimed incredulously, his mind slipping back to his boyhood in this town, and to the small blonde schoolgirl who had followed him around.

She laughed. "I've changed, haven't I?"

"You certainly have!" he smiled.

"She's done well for herself," Mrs. Craig interjected proudly. "She's engaged to Ralph Bellamy."

Stephen noticed the girl's quick frown. Then, as if in answer to a cue, a slightly built young fellow with light brown hair, came up to them.

Stephen recognized him as Henry Bellamy's son, recognized also the manner in which he took Wendy's arm and with barely a word led her away. Mrs. Craig appeared to be about to make some comment, when the color suddenly drained from her face, and a look of dismay came into her eyes.

Following her glance, Stephen could perceive no reason for this change.

"I'll see you again, Mr. Thornton," she said abstractedly, moving away.

Stephen turned to accept a cup of tea from Anne Ogden, only to have it almost knocked out of his hand as a girl elbowed her way to his side.

Remembering how surprised he had been by Wendy's appearance, he tried to think if the newcomer had been one of his former friends. But the unruly crown of auburn hair, and the frankly curious hazel eyes, refused to stir any memories.

"I'm Catherine Williams of the *Redford Gazette,*" she introduced herself. "I'm here to report tonight's activities, Mr. Thornton. I wondered if there was a brief personal message you wished me to include."

Stephen took her extended hand, surprised by the strength of its grip. "Glad to meet you, Miss Williams," he responded. "No. I don't think there's anything to add."

"Nothing on this—family angle?" she persisted. "I'm a comparative newcomer to Redford, but I've gathered your arrival has caused quite a stir. There was rather a—dramatic situation concerning your father, I believe. Wouldn't you like to make some comment on your decision to return here in the light of it? It would give a new slant to a routine report."

He looked at her in growing distaste. "I'm not concerned with digging up the past, Miss Williams," he told her curtly, "only in building up the future. I came here to do God's work, and that's the only comment I'm prepared to make." At this juncture someone else tried to get his attention, and he turned away from Catherine in relief.

Soon afterwards Mrs. Ogden approached, bringing with her a harassed looking woman, followed by two girls.

"This is Mrs. Wilson, our next door neighbor," she explained. "They moved to Redford just after—you left."

It was evident to Stephen that this woman had known trouble. The girl immediately behind her, an outlandishly dressed teenager, looking up at him from between curtains of straight dark hair, was introduced as her daughter, Jennifer.

11

"And this is Jean Collins," Mrs. Wilson indicated the other girl. "She's only just come to Redford, and she's lodging with us."

Stephen saw that he was face to face with the girl who had arrived after the service had started. She was very attractive, with dark eyes, regular features and a clear creamy skin. An air of cool detachment set her apart from the talkative gathering. He sensed that she was not interested in the gathering and he wondered why she had come. And yet in spite of her self-sufficient attitude, there was a sadness in her face which troubled him.

She moved away, and Hubert Craig touched his arm saying apologetically, "I hope you won't mind if we leave now, Mr. Thornton. My wife isn't feeling very well."

"I'm sorry," Stephen rejoined, recollecting Mrs. Craig's strained appearance. "There's no need for you to wait," he assured the deacon. "Everyone will be leaving soon."

CHAPTER TWO

Hubert Craig took his wife's arm, and led her to where their car was parked. When she had begged him to take her home, her face had been deathly white, her hands shaking.

"What's the matter?" he asked her gently. "You look as if you've seen a ghost."

"Perhaps I have!" she answered unevenly.

"You mean the ghost of that old childhood romance between our Wendy and Stephen Thornton," he said. "Well—you don't have to worry about that. Wendy's safely engaged to Ralph, and even if she weren't she wouldn't go for a poorly paid minister. You've trained her too well!"

She was aware of the irony underlying the softly spoken words. Over the years, for all his gentleness and consideration, Hubert had taken her measure. He had been alternately amused and annoyed by her efforts to bring Ralph and Wendy together. It was all right for Hubert to smile at her ambition for Wendy. Born into the comfortably-fixed Craig family, he had never known what it was to go short of things.

She felt a glow of satisfaction as she compared her daughter's position with her own at Wendy's age. Hubert's family had expected him to marry a girl from a certain type of background, and Eleanor, a newcomer to Redford, had manufactured such a way of life. But now the face in the crowd brought to life her real past.

Soon after the Craigs had left the Chapel, Henry Bellamy also excused himself. His wife, Rita, who had endured the whole evening with an air of polite boredom, collected her fur coat, and followed her husband out of the building.

She was a Londoner and had met Henry, then a widower, when he had been in the city on business. After they had fallen in love, he had taken her home to introduce her to Ralph, the son of his first marriage. She hadn't realized how dull she would find life in the northern industrial town. But her genuine admiration for Henry had never wavered. She had sensed that he would get to the top, and he had amply justified her faith. Two years after their marriage, he had been appointed manager of the Albion Mill, and they had bought Hillcrest, the large imposing house they were now approaching on the top of the gradual rise from the town. She did not realize that her husband's position was threatened by Stephen's return, and endured his moody silence on the drive home.

The crowd in the Chapel schoolroom was thinning out now. Ralph took Wendy's arm, suggesting that they go for a drive.

She agreed indifferently, but her first remark showed that her thoughts were still with the minister. "Stephen carried it off marvelously well," she said. "It must have been difficult for him in the circumstances, but then—he never lacked courage."

"He obviously had you eating out of his hand," Ralph returned sarcastically. "Need you have been so effusive? You were little more than children when last you met."

"I wish you wouldn't be so jealous," Wendy sighed. "I can't go around ignoring everyone just because I belong to you, can I?"

Ralph silently treasured her 'I belong to you'. There were times when he wondered if Wendy did really belong to him. He had never recovered from his astonishment that she had promised to marry him. The root of his sense of inferiority lay in the knowledge that he was a disappointment to his father. He hadn't inherited a bit of Henry Bellamy's dominating personality. He had deferred meekly to his father's wishes, even when it had come to the choice of a career. He had been pushed into working at the Albion Mill, although he disliked the trade intensely. He was now a foreman, very conscious of the fact that it was only his father's influence which had gained him the position.

Wendy, sensing the nature of his thoughts, felt sorry for him. Half the time Ralph's attitude exasperated her, and then when she'd snap at him, he would look at her with the expression of a small scolded boy, and she would feel protective and responsible. She often wondered whether this kind of affection was enough to base a marriage on, and had tried to talk to her mother about it, but Mrs. Craig had dismissed her doubts as due to 'pre-wedding nerves'.

"Let's drive round by the house," Ralph suggested.

Ralph was thrilled with the new house that was to be his parents' wedding gift and he would drive past it on every possible occasion.

A few minutes later they reached the housing estate outside the town. "Look!" he exclaimed eagerly, "They've started work on the roof. Let's walk up our garden path!"

Together he and Wendy picked their way over the uneven ground toward the oblong gap that would eventually be their front door. He wanted to give her so much, she thought, the familiar wave of tenderness sweeping through her. She must do everything within her power to make him happy. When Ralph took her in his arms, she responded to his kiss, trying to shut out the persistent memory of Stephen Thornton.

Jean Collins walked across from the Chapel with Mrs. Wilson and Jennifer. Her head was whirling from having been introduced to so many people within the space of one hour.

"I think you've met everybody!" Jennifer stated with satisfaction.

"I'm sure she has!" Mary Wilson smiled wryly at Jean. "I should think the poor girl's bewildered."

Jean smiled. "It was kind of you to go out of your way to make me feel at home," she answered.

Jennifer shrugged. "I'll do the same for you at the mill on Monday. I meet everyone—being in Mr. Bellamy's office. The other typists are nice, but watch out for Miss Blake, Mr. Bellamy's secretary. She's a regular dragon! She wanted to get her claws on him after his first wife died. She's been sour ever since he married that woman from London."

"That's enough, Jennifer!" her mother reprimanded sharply, as she opened the front door.

She followed Jennifer into the living room, where her father was watching television. He barely glanced at them. Jean's sympathy was extended to Mary Wilson. Her husband was disabled, so Jennifer had informed her, as the result of an auto accident. His inability to earn a living had made him bitter, and unfortunately, he took out on his family. He was humiliated because that his wife had to take on a part time job in one of the shops, and had decided to rent the spare bedroom.

15

Jean felt tired and stating that she would have an early night, reached the foot of the stairs as Roy, Jennifer's elder brother, came in through the front door.

"Hello! Tea and bun fight over then?" he queried.

"Yes," she smiled.

"I suppose you're fagged out. That's the effect Chapel affairs always had on me when I used to go. Don't let Jenny bully you into them if you're not really interested."

"She didn't. I enjoyed it," Jean replied walking on upstairs.

She was aware of the interest and admiration in Roy's dark eyes, but she had no intention of encouraging him. Nothing was going to distract her from the purpose that had brought her to Redford!

CHAPTER THREE

When Stephen entered the Chapel on Sunday morning, he saw that it was almost full. He was nervous, although he managed not to show it. He realized that many of these people remembered his grandfather's eloquence, and would set a high standard for him.

As he had prepared for this morning's service, the parable of the sower had come continually into his mind.

Redford was indeed stony ground. The people sat stiffly at attention, their eyes fixed dutifully upon Stephen, but he knew he wasn't getting through to them. He was up against complacency and indifference.

He remembered the meetings of his boyhood, people seeking salvation, the hymns and prayers springing from their hearts. He recalled his grandfather's words: "There can be no harvest of souls unless the seed of God's Word is sown with tears and heart hunger for their salvation. There can be no crop unless the ground is first broken up and ploughed, and that can be a very painful process."

After the service he went to the door to shake hands with the people. The Ogdens remarked that his sermon had been just what Blakelock Hill Chapel needed. Mary Wilson's tired face was illumined with an inner joy, as though a fire had been rekindled that had been burning low for a long time, but Jean Collins still had the same detached expression on her face.

They were closely followed by the girl reporter from the *Redford Gazette*.

"Is this another official visit, Miss Williams?" he greeted her, his smile tempering his words, for he felt he had been more curt than necessary with her the previous night. After all, she had only been doing her job.

She returned the smile, relieved to find his attitude more friendly. "No. This is purely personal," she replied. "I was curious to see what you'd make of this first Sunday morning service."

"And what's the verdict?" he asked.

There was confusion in her hazel eyes, and something else, too. Surprised, he realized that the service had affected her deeply.

"It's difficult to put into words," she confessed. "I've never been in the habit of attending Chapel, but—I think I'll come again."

At this juncture they were joined by a tall fair-haired young man. He evidently knew Catherine well. "I never thought to see you here," he stated. "I suppose this is overtime!"

"I've already explained to Mr. Thorton that my visit's quite unofficial," she stated and hurried away.

There was an awkward pause. "I'm sorry to have hurt her feelings," the young man explained to Stephen, "but usually Catherine goes to a great deal of trouble trying to make people believe she hasn't any! I didn't think she could be here other than to report your first service for her paper. I was sorry I couldn't make it last night," he continued. "I was called out. I'm Doctor Waring, Donald Waring to you. I'm glad about your appointment. This place needs livening up. You can count on my support."

"Thanks," Stephen answered gratefully.

After lunch Stephen decided to go for a walk. He made his way along the road which led from Redford to Brentwood at the other end of the valley. Gradually the houses thinned out, until only an occasional farm or cottage bordered the road.

He passed a large garage bearing the sign "Wayside Filling Station. Proprietor—Ernest Briggs," and a short distance beyond this the road forked. To the left he could go on to Brentwood, to the right a narrowing lane led back into Redford through the woods which bordered this side of the town.

Stephen followed the lane. He walked slowly, enjoying the peaceful scene. Then with a sense of disappointment, he realized that he didn't have the woods to himself, after all. Jean Collins was walking ahead of him. Although he wasn't in the mood for conversation, Stephen realized he could not pass her without some comment.

She turned at the sound of his footsteps, and he was troubled by the look of bleak unhappiness on her face.

"Getting acquainted with one of the local beauty spots, Miss Collins?" he greeted her.

"Yes," she answered falling into step beside him. "It's lovely through here. I wanted to be somewhere quiet for a while. I don't seem to have had a minute to myself since I arrived. Everyone's been very kind, though, trying to make me feel at home. Jennifer Wilson's a dear," she smiled, "but she can be a bit overwhelming. When she tried to rope me into helping her at Sunday school this afternoon, I got out of it by explaining that I've never been a Chapel-goer, and would hardly qualify to teach Scripture to young children."

"Yet you were at the Chapel—twice?" Stephen remarked curiously.

She laughed. "Mrs. Wilson and Jennifer seemed keen to get me to the service last night, partly, I think, because of the social afterwards. They thought it would give me an opportunity of meeting people. At first I refused, and then after they'd left home, I felt guilty, so I followed on.

"Then this morning, they just seemed to take it for granted that I was going with them, so I fell in with the idea. I don't know why. My purpose in coming to Redford isn't conducive to listening to sermons!"

Something in her voice filled Stephen with a sense of disquiet. Underneath her even tones there was a bitterness that troubled him.

"What part of the country are you from?" he asked her.

"A small town in the midlands. I wanted to get away. You see my mother died recently."

"I'm sorry," he murmured sympathetically. This was the reason for her unhappiness, he reflected. He had encountered a similar bitterness in other people when they could not come to terms with their loss. This girl certainly needed the comfort and help of the Christian faith, and he resolved to do everything he could to recommend it to her.

"You were wise in making a clean break," he told her.

"It was the only thing to do," she answered. "And tomorrow I'm starting as a typist at the Albion Mill, so there won't be time for brooding on the past."

They had come to the point where the path crossed the road which wound through Redford.

"I must get back now," Stephen remarked, glancing at his watch.

"I'll go on through the woods," she replied. "I've an hour to spare before tea."

"If you keep to that path," he pointed straight ahead, "it will bring you out at the far end of the town."

As he was directing her, a small blue sports car shot past them, and Stephen had a swift glimpse of Wendy Craig and Ralph Bellamy.

Jean glanced briefly at the car, and then turned back to him, "I'll find the way, Mr. Thornton," she assured him, and set off along the path which he had pointed out. Stephen turned and retraced his steps back to his lodgings.

In the car Wendy Craig's face wore a disappointed frown. She had been all set to enjoy the afternoon drive with Ralph, when they had caught sight of Stephen Thornton talking to that dark girl who had just come to Redford. She hadn't wasted much time in making his acquaintance, Wendy reflected jealously.

Ralph, concentrating upon his driving, hadn't recognized the young couple, but Wendy's short replies to his remarks at last prompted him to ask in exasperation, "What's gotten into you? Have I said something to upset you?"

"I've got a headache," Wendy hedged. She knew it would be playing with fire to let Ralph get an inkling of the real reason for her irritation. It was too soon after the argument they'd had last night about Stephen Thornton. She would have to fight this pointless absorption with the young minister. Her future was bound up with Ralph's. It was too late to back out of the arrangement now!

CHAPTER FOUR

Redford was bustling in its usual Monday morning activity when Catherine Williams left her flat on High Street, and made her way to the *Gazette* Office. She replied abstractedly to the greetings of her fellow workers in the old-fashioned building, and went directly to the Editor's office.

"This is routine stuff!" Ted Ellis complained when he had glanced through her report on the installation service. "I wanted something different, based on the Thornton family's associations with the town."

"I'm sorry, Mr. Ellis," Catherine answered in an unusually subdued voice. "I tried to get Stephen Thornton to comment on the family angle, but he refused. He doesn't want the past dug up," she paused and added impulsively, "he's above letting us use the old story as a gimmick to give an initial impetus to his work, and a new interest to our pages."

"Oh, he is, is he!" Ted Ellis returned sarcastically. "You're supposed to be able to handle all sorts of people—reticent preachers included! What's wrong with you? Getting scrupulous about your methods?"

Catherine hesitated, and he was struck by the new composure about her. He had expected the familiar flash of anger at his criticism. He was puzzled. He'd given her some tough assignments in the past, and usually she'd managed to crack them wide open.

"I wrote what I believed I ought to write," she explained. "I'm sorry if you're not satisfied, but Mr. Thornton's not the kind of man you use like that. I believe his motives in coming back are exactly what he declared them to be—as I've recorded them."

21

Her boss stared at her incredulously. "He seems to have made an impression on you!" he declared.

Later that morning a small, shabbily dressed man crossed from Redford Station to the Albion Mill.

He paused and looked up at the tall building, its grimy chimney belching out a trail of smoke across the pale spring sky, and a smile of satisfaction crossed his wrinkled, monkey-like features.

Approaching the office entrance, he tapped on the Enquiries window. The young girl who opened it, a newcomer to Redford, stared at him in astonishment when he asked to speak to Mr. Bellamy. Thinking that he was some 'down and out' in search of a job, she said stiffly, "Mr. Bellamy doesn't see anyone without an appointment. If you're looking for work, you'll have to fill in an application form."

He seemed to find her remarks amusing, for he laughed as he assured her, "I don't want a job! I want a few words with Mr. Bellamy. If you'll inform him that Bill Jennings is here, you'll find he'll see me right away!"

The girl studied him unbelievingly for a few seconds before phoning the manager's office. Then she returned to the window. "His secretary says you're to go straight up," she stated in a bewildered voice. "His office is the first on the right."

"I know where it is, thanks," he responded.

Miss Blake ushered Jennings into the office and told him to go straight into Mr. Bellamy's room.

Closing the door of the manager's office firmly behind him, she returned to her desk and sat down in front of her typewriter.

Jennifer looked up from her filing. "Fancy that odd Mr. Jennings turning up again!" she exclaimed curiously, glancing at Miss Blake.

"It's not for you to comment on Mr. Bellamy's visitors, my girl!" Ethel Blake replied curtly, "Get on with your work."

Jennifer began filing again, and Miss Blake began typing as though her life depended upon it.

Jennifer would have been even more intrigued had she been able to see Jennings' effect on Henry Bellamy. He was slumped in his chair, his normally florid face grey and drawn.

"What do you want?" he asked Jennings brusquely.

"What I usually want when I come to see you," he replied. "Times are hard, the cost of living's gone up, and I've nothing left."

22

"I told you last time you can't keep on making these demands. You're not going to sponge on me forever," Bellamy said thickly.

"I haven't troubled you for some time," Jennings returned easily. "I was getting homesick for the old place. I'm not the only one to return, either. I hear young Thornton's back."

"You're a parasite!" Bellamy leaned forward, gripping the edge of his desk.

"And you, Councilman Bellamy," Jennings stressed the name sarcastically, "are a very important man. Isn't your continued good name worth the price of my silence?"

The mill manager got up from his chair and moved to the window. Below in the yard the warehouse laborers were slinging the heavy skips of yarn on to a waiting truck. The hum of the looms in the spinning rooms reached his ears with the regular rhythm that had become as much a part of his life as his own pulse beat.

"How much do you want?" Bellamy said wearily.

"About fifty pounds—in cash," his visitor replied.

Henry unlocked his desk, and counted out forty-five pounds. "That's all I have on hand," he said.

Jennings' hands fastened around the notes. "Thanks," he said, getting to his feet. "I'll make it last as long as I can."

Henry didn't answer. He slumped back in his chair, aware of the tremendous strain the interview had put upon him. As Jennings went out the room began to spin around him.

Jennifer had a glimpse of him through the partly open door. Miss Blake went in to her employer, closing the door behind her.

Quickly she reached for the bottle of tablets which Henry kept in his desk. He took them gratefully, swallowed one and sat forward, his head supported on his hands. Ethel Blake watched in silent concern. She'd seen these symptoms before, and knew how to cope with them. Usually they followed some particularly difficult problem or dispute connected with the running of the mill. This one, she knew, was caused by Jennings' visit. He had worked spasmodically at the mill in her younger days, and then drifted out of the town, coming back for brief visits. During recent years she had noticed the adverse effect his visits had on Mr. Bellamy, and had wondered why he agreed to see the man. As a rule he was forceful enough in getting rid of difficult characters.

She saw that he was beginning to recover, and put the tablets away, aware that he didn't want anyone else to know about these attacks. If that woman from London, as Ethel Blake classified Rita Bellamy, had any sense, she'd see that her husband was working too hard, and make him ease up. But Rita was too obsessed with her bridge parties, her golf, and her trips into the city to buy new clothes, to notice that Henry wasn't well.

There was an unusual tenderness in Ethel Blake's face as she looked down at her employer. When he'd married for the second time, why hadn't he chosen an ordinary hard working woman from a background similar to his own, she wondered.

As though aware of her scrutiny, Henry looked up. "I'm all right now, thank you, Miss Blake," he said quietly, and she knew she was being dismissed.

At lunch Jennifer met Jean Collins. She had insisted upon taking the new girl to the canteen, and Jean, still feeling strange in her new surroundings, was glad of her company.

"How did it go?" Jennifer asked her.

"All right," Jean answered. "I can manage the work. I think I shall enjoy the job when I've settled down."

"It would help you to get really involved in things if you joined the Chapel," Jennifer said as they were eating. "There's always something going on there. The youth fellowship social is on Thursday night. You must come with me."

Jean laughed. "You're very surprising!" she stated. "You don't strike me as a Chapel type at all."

"I'm no goody-goody," Jennifer admitted frankly. "I don't listen to the sermons. I just sit and plan my new outfits, or think about my next date. It's the social activities I go for. Redford's dead, and I can't stand staying in the house. Dad's such a wet blanket. Promise me you'll come on Thursday?"

"All right," Jean smiled. "I can't really get out of it!"

Jean was glad when five o'clock came and the first day was over. She walked back with Jennifer, and the girl's words about her father being a wet blanket returned to her as they sat down for their meal. Jim Wilson barely acknowledged any of them.

Jennifer, however, made a determined effort to draw him into the conversation. "Something queer happened at work today, Dad," she announced. "That horrid little man, Jennings, called. Remember the one who worked with you at the mill when we first came here."

24

"Oh!" For the first time Jean detected a note of interest in Jim Wilson's voice. "What did he want?"

"He demanded to see Mr. Bellamy. So Yvonne at the reception desk told me. Marched up to the big chief's office as though he owned the place. I couldn't hear what they said, but when Jennings left, I caught a glimpse of Mr. Bellamy and he looked really ill."

"What goes on at the office is confidential," Mrs. Wilson reprimanded.

"What goes on there concerns me, too," her husband growled. "Haven't I a score to settle with Henry Bellamy? Haven't I him to thank for this?" he banged the arms of his wheelchair viciously.

Mary sighed. All conversations led back to the subject of Jim's disability.

He had stepped off the pavement coming home from the mill in the rush hour, and been knocked down by Henry Bellamy, who was driving home. There had been compensation, of course, but no amount of compensation was adequate to cover the loss of his self-respect now that he could no longer earn a living. Later, when he had recovered as much as it seemed he was likely to do, he had applied to Henry Bellamy for a sedentary job, but the mill manager had stated that there was no vacancy which Jim could suitably fill. Ever since, Jim had cherished the desire to get even with him.

"Keep your eyes and ears open," he told his daughter. "If Jennings calls again, ask him to come and see me. If he's got some hold over Henry Bellamy, I'd like to know what it is."

"Jim," his wife intervened, "please don't get involved in anything that will bring us more trouble. There's no future in brooding over it and trying to get your own back."

"You'd rather go on putting up with things and praying about them!" he returned sarcastically. "Show me the kind of future there is in that!"

Mary didn't answer, and Jean saw the sudden look of pain in her eyes as she hurried out to the kitchen. At first the family dispute had merely embarrassed Jean. Then she began to wonder if this bitter man could help her with the enquiries which had brought to Redford. She waited until Roy and Jennifer had gone out, and Mary Wilson was ironing in the kitchen. Then, during the television commercials, she began tentatively, "Mr. Wilson, you've been in Redford several years. You must know most of the people by now."

"What of it?" he asked shortly.

"I'm trying to trace someone. It's rather a hopeless search, as I don't know what she looks like, or even her present surname. Her Christian name is Nell. That's all I have to go off, apart from this." She took a piece of newspaper from her handbag and spread it out in front of him. Jim Wilson looked at a faded photograph of a group of women wearing the kind of overalls used by munition workers in World War II. Underneath was the caption, "Workers from local factory organize concert in aid of Red Cross." It had been cut from the *Redford Gazette* in 1943.

"You're going back a bit, aren't you?" he commented drily.

"All the way back!" Jean's eyes clouded. "Is there anyone you recognize, Mr. Wilson?"

"I'm afraid not. We've only been here six years. These people have aged since the time this photograph was taken. And since you don't know the full name, it makes it difficult."

"Almost impossible," she agreed. "And yet—I must find her!"

He looked at her with a new interest, reading in the shadows in her young face a hint of his own bitterness. "I'm sorry I can't help you, lass," he said.

Jean folded the picture away. "Well, thanks anyway for trying, Mr. Wilson," she said. "I'll just have to keep on looking."

CHAPTER FIVE

Between them Wendy Craig and Ralph Bellamy ran the Blake-lock Hill Youth Fellowship. Its various enterprises were usually well supported, because there was hardly anywhere else in Redford for the youngsters to go. But, as Stephen Thornton soon realized, there was no real spiritual life among the young people.

At the Youth Fellowship Ralph was in his element. The sense of inferiority which dogged him at the mill vanished. He had a natural aptitude for dealing with young people, and it was evident that this crowd thought the world of him. Stephen moved among them Thursday night, unaware of the way in which Wendy was watching him.

She was brought back to her official duties as Jennifer Wilson touched her arm. "I've brought Jean Collins with me," she introduced her companion.

Wendy studied the dark, reserved-looking girl in silence. Once again she was seeing Stephen by Jean's side on the woodland road. Aware of the hostility in Wendy's glance, Jean was puzzled. After all they had never really met. It wasn't until she noticed the expression on Wendy's face as she watched the young minister, that a possible explanation for her attitude dawned upon Jean. She remembered the sports car that had passed by on Sunday when Stephen Thornton had been directing her through the woods. She had recognized Wendy and Ralph, and thought no more of the incident. But obviously Wendy had! It was evident she resented his friendliness toward Jean. Yet Wendy was engaged to Ralph! Why should she be so taken with Stephen Thornton? Jean was suddenly amused by the whole situation. Wendy needn't worry, she thought wryly. She was too interested in other things to be interested in the minister.

When he left the school that night, Stephen walked down Blakelock Hill to the old-fashioned house on the corner where Doctors G. Gilmore and D. Waring held surgery. Stephen had met Donald Waring during the week, and the young doctor had asked him to call after the social.

Doctor Gilmore and his wife had moved out of the old house into a smaller one outside the town. He was soon to retire, and Donald would then take over the practice.

A moment or so after Stephen had pressed the front doorbell, Donald appeared, still wearing his overcoat.

"Have you been called out?" Stephen asked him.

"No. I've just got back from Hillcrest. I had to go and see Mr. Bellamy. Let's go up to the fire."

He led the way to his living room, and switched on the large electric fire. Stephen flung off his coat and sat down in one of the comfortable chairs.

"What's wrong with Mr. Bellamy?" he enquired.

"He collapsed after dinner tonight. It was a terrible shock to his wife. Apparently she didn't know he'd been having treatment for months. He does too much. He's no longer a young man."

"His wife thinks something is worrying him," Donald went on. "I told him to stay at home and rest for a few days, but—he's a very stubborn man."

"I know!" Stephen agreed wryly. "I'll call in on him." He didn't tell Donald that he was not relishing the prospect, remembering Henry's cold unwelcoming manner. He had since coupled it with the stray, well-meant warnings some of his people had given him that Bellamy had opposed his appointment.

"And how do you feel about your work, after your first few days here?" Donald asked him.

"I haven't even touched the surface of it yet," Stephen admitted. "It's a granite-tough one, too. It will need prayer and self-sacrifice and every bit of endeavor of which I'm capable, backed by the power of God, to enable me to break through, but—I won't be satisfied with anything less than revival!"

"Revival—in these days!" Donald exclaimed incredulously.

"Why not? The power of God hasn't diminished. It only needs His people to fulfill the conditions."

"That's a tremendous 'if,' " the doctor responded. "Basically the religious life of Redford is all on the surface. Church attendance is only a habit—a good habit, but—Christ demands so much more."

"And it's because of His challenge that I'm here," Stephen returned.

"Well," Donald reminded him, "in Matthew it says, 'if two of you shall agree on earth as touching anything that they shall ask, it shall be done for them of my Father which is in heaven.' Maybe you and I could be the beginning of a revival by praying for it together."

"That's exactly what I was hoping you'd say," Stephen responded.

The next day Stephen called at Hillcrest.

Rita Bellamy let Stephen in.

"Mr. Thornton! We weren't expecting you!" she exclaimed. Her tone made Stephen feel as if he should have first made an appointment.

"I heard your husband wasn't very well," he told her.

"He isn't, I'm afraid. Come in!" She led the way across the thickly carpeted hall, and opened a door on the right.

Stephen followed her into a large, beautifully furnished room. Henry Bellamy was leaning back in one of the deep armchairs. His immediate frown told Stephen that he wasn't welcome.

"Sit down, Mr. Thornton," Rita Bellamy invited him. "I'll make some coffee."

As she left the room, he turned to her husband. "I was sorry to hear of your illness, Mr. Bellamy," he began.

"I suppose young Waring told you," Henry replied acidly. "Ordering me to stay at home and rest! As if I can!"

It was obvious that he was suffering from nervous tension. Stephen looked around the room. It was ironic—a man possessing all the means necessary for comfortable living, and yet not being able to live comfortably with himself!

"I don't suppose the doctor will keep you at home any longer than he believes necessary," he assured Bellamy.

The mill manager made an effort to control his feelings, telling himself that it was ridiculous to be so put out by the minister's visit. Some of his self-confidence returned when his wife came back with the coffee.

"Well, Mr. Thornton, what are your impressions of the work?" he asked. "You've taken on a difficult task! We've had any num-

29

ber of ministers, and not one of them was able to make much headway."

"So I've been told," Stephen replied. "I know what I've taken on, Mr. Bellamy, and I know that God is able to give victory in this place."

"It was hardly fair to you, though, young and inexperienced, being sent to a place like this," Bellamy pursued.

"Actually I have great hopes for the work here," Stephen countered quietly. "I was telling Doctor Waring last night, I'm praying and preparing for revival."

The big man smiled slightly, as a mature adult will smile at a child who announces that he is going to perform an absurdly impossible feat.

"Revival!" he echoed. "That's an outdated word! I don't think you'll find the people of Redford so easily swayed by their emotions as they were in the days you're remembering. They are better educated now; they like to reason things out logically."

"They still need God," Stephen answered. "And with Him all things are possible. We have no right to limit His power."

For an instant their eyes met in mutual challenge. It was Henry Bellamy who looked away.

Stephen put down his empty cup and got to his feet. "I must go now," he told them. "I've several other calls to make. Thanks for the coffee."

Rita Bellamy went with him to the front door. When she returned to the lounge, her husband was watching him go down the drive, an inscrutable expression on his face. She wondered why the minister's visit had so disturbed Henry, and in an effort to persuade him to confide in her, she remarked, "You certainly tried to pour cold water on Mr. Thornton's schemes!"

"I was trying to let him down lightly," he responded, "to save him from the inevitable disappointment the others have had to face."

With a sigh, Rita stacked the cups and saucers on to the tray. During the last day or two she had tried to discover what was worrying Henry, but he refused to confide in her. If only he'd let her really share his life, she wouldn't be so bored with Redford.

CHAPTER SIX

About three weeks later, during her lunch hour Jean Collins made her way to the offices of the *Gazette*. In her handbag was the photograph which she had shown to Jim Wilson. She was hoping that someone at the newspaper office would be able to identify the people in the picture and tell her if any of them were still in the town.

She reached the entrance at the same time Catherine Williams did. Recognizing Jean, Catherine gave her a friendly smile. "Coming in here?" she asked.

Jean nodded and Catherine asked, "What is it? An advertisement?"

Jean hesitated, realizing now how strange her request would seem. "No. It's something rather unusual," she answered.

Catherine's ready curiosity was aroused. One of the girls usually on duty at the advertisement counter had gone to lunch. Her assistant at the other end was already fully occupied.

"Perhaps I can help you?" Catherine suggested.

Jean fished out the newspaper photograph, and repeated the explanation she had given to Jim Wilson.

Catherine studied the picture thoughtfully. "It's a long time ago," she said. "If you'd like to hang on a minute, I'll make some enquiries."

Jean thanked her and passed the time watching the different people who came in. Stephen Thornton was one of them. He gave her a friendly smile and asked her if she was settling down all right.

"Yes. Redford's not bad," she conceded. Then as she saw the line at the other end of the counter dwindling, she told him, "I

31

think you'll get attended to down there, if it's about an advertisement. I'm waiting for something else."

"Oh, I see," he moved away, and almost immediately Catherine returned.

"I'm afraid I can't be of much help," she said. "Our records don't give the identity of these people, and no one seems able to recognize them. It's such an old photograph. All I can tell you is that it was taken outside a factory which was destroyed by fire years ago. I'm afraid the firm is no longer in existence, so you can't follow up your enquiries there."

Jean gave a disappointed sigh. "Well—you've done all you can to help," she said quietly. "Thanks very much."

She turned to leave just as Stephen moved away from the counter. He held the door open for her, noticing her despondent expression.

Impulsively she remarked, "Do you ever feel as if you're up against a blank wall?"

"Quite frequently!" he assured her.

Aware of the sympathetic interest in his face, she almost took him into her confidence regarding her business in the *Gazette* office. Then, abruptly she changed her mind. It was not likely that Stephen would be able to help her in her enquiries, since he was only about the same age as she was, and would not know anyone on such an old photograph.

Sensing that she did not wish to talk about her business in the *Gazette* office, Stephen remarked conversationally, "I've just been handing in an advertisement about some special meetings we're holding. I've approached several other ministers in the town, and found them quite enthusiastic about the idea of a joint evangelical campaign later in the year. We shall pool our resources and rent a large hall in the town center. We hope to draw in those people who don't attend any place of worship, and at the same time to deepen the spiritual life of our members. There's a lot of work to be done first, and I'm having a series of preparatory meetings in our own Chapel during the next few weeks."

Jean smiled to herself. He certainly wasn't one to let grass grow under his feet! He hadn't been in Redford a month, and already he was agitating for an evangelical campaign.

On the street corner they bumped into Roy Wilson. Stephen greeted him easily. He was trying to make contact with Roy, but

32

the young man was deeply antagonistic towards anyone connected with religion.

"I must hurry back to the mill," Jean remarked. "My lunch hour's over."

"I'm going that way," Roy said instantly. "Mr. Briggs," he named the owner of the Wayside Garage, where he was a mechanic, "has run out of spares, and he's sent me into town for them. My motor bike's across the road."

They said good-by to Stephen and crossed the busy thoroughfare together.

That evening Jim Wilson was alone in the house. He heard a loud knock above the noise of the television.

He called "Come in," and was surprised when Bill Jennings appeared.

"Your lass said you wanted to see me," he announced.

"Yes. Come and sit down. Turn that thing off," Jim indicated the television set.

Jennings obeyed. "I came at the first opportunity," he said. "I haven't been back in Redford very long."

"Long enough to get your hooks into Henry Bellamy!" Jim answered.

"What do you mean?" Jennings looked offended.

"Come off it, Bill! When young Jenny told me you'd visited Bellamy, and the effect you'd had on him, I guessed what was going on. You're putting the squeeze on him, aren't you?"

Jennings laughed. "If so, am I likely to take you into my confidence?"

"We're old mates," Jim's voice was pathetically eager. "I've vowed for years that I'd get even with Bellamy for where I am now."

"The one snag is that you're in a tight corner," Jennings replied evenly. "You couldn't pay me for the information."

"You'd take money from me—in my circumstances!" Jim spluttered indignantly.

"I wouldn't like to," Jennings answered, with an over-acted sincerity. "But this information is too valuable to give away."

"I'll remember this!" Jim glowered at him.

"I'm sorry," Jennings got to his feet. "We won't say the deal is closed. You may find a way out—or young Roy may," he finished.

"Roy! What made you mention him?" Jim queried anxiously.

33

"We're working together. Hasn't he told you?" Jennings explained.

"You leave Roy out of this," Jim threatened.

Jennings laughed as he made for the door. "Don't worry, Jim," he stated. "Your son can take care of himself. I'll see you again."

He was letting himself out as Mary came down the path. "What's that man been here for?" she asked, seeing that Jim looked upset.

"You heard me tell Jenny to ask him to call," he answered briefly.

"Jim, please don't get involved with him," she pleaded. "There was always trouble whenever he appeared. Don't you think we've had enough?"

"Of course I do! I'm trying to think of a way out of our troubles," he retorted.

"Well he won't provide it," she answered.

He lapsed into silence, and she went into the kitchen to prepare supper. Deliberately she turned her thoughts away from Jim's unpleasant visitor to the prayer meeting she had just left. It had been different from the meetings she had attended before Stephen Thornton had come to Redford. He had prayed for revival, and she, too, had silently joined in that prayer, knowing it was the only answer to her family problems.

CHAPTER SEVEN

It was Wendy Craig's habit, as leader of the girls' section of the Youth Fellowship, to invite any new members to her home for tea. Wendy felt that it was time she asked Jean to Fairview, but she kept putting it off because of her antagonism towards the older girl. She admitted that it stemmed from the moment when she had seen Jean talking to Stephen Thornton in the woods. She had glimpsed them together on another occasion, too, coming out of the *Gazette* Office. But when she realized that her attitude was becoming apparent to the other members of the Youth Fellowship Wendy made a special effort, and invited Jean to her home one Saturday at the end of April.

"Do you play tennis?" she asked.

Jean nodded.

"Good," Wendy replied. "We have a tennis court, and if this nice weather holds out we'll be able to have a game."

And so Saturday afternoon Jean went to Fairview. As she turned in at the wrought iron gates, Jean saw Wendy coming to meet her, Blackie, her pet poodle at her heels.

The little dog made a great fuss of the visitor, and Jean gave him plenty of attention. His presence bridged the awkward first few minutes that the two girls were together.

"You'd better come in and say 'Hello' to Mum first, before we go round to the tennis court," Wendy said as they walked up the drive. "She'll have a cup of tea ready for us."

The front door was open, and Mrs. Craig came into the hall to welcome her daughter's visitor. Then she stopped abruptly, the smile freezing on her lips, and the color draining from her cheeks.

"Mum, this is Jean Collins," Wendy began, and stopped as she

35

saw her mother's expression. She was staring at the newcomer as if she had seen a ghost!

"What's the matter? Do you feel ill?" Wendy asked her.

Eleanor Craig composed herself with an effort. "I'm all right. Just a headache," she explained, coming forward to take Jean's hand. "I'm pleased to meet you, dear," she said stiffly. "Now, if you two would like to go into the lounge, I'll bring you some tea."

"Let me make it if you don't feel well," Wendy offered.

"No, dear, thanks all the same," her mother insisted. "There's something I must attend to in the kitchen."

Closing the door behind her, she leaned against it, aware that she was still trembling. When Wendy had announced that she was inviting a friend home, she had simply said that the girl worked at the Albion Mill, and had recently started attending the Youth Fellowship.

Abruptly, as though the movement would banish the specters, she crossed the kitchen, and began setting cups and saucers on the tray. She must keep calm. She mustn't give herself away again, as she had almost done a few minutes ago. Perhaps she was mistaken. Maybe this girl's resemblance to the face that had haunted her throughout the years, was just one of those chance likenesses. So Eleanor tried to reassure herself, realizing that it was indeed an uncanny coincidence that this girl should have the same Christian name.

At last she forced herself to walk towards the lounge.

"Are you all right now?" Wendy asked.

"Yes, thanks," Eleanor returned briefly. "Drink your tea, and then you'll have time for a game of tennis before our evening meal."

Jean took the dainty cup and saucer, thanking her hostess, and Eleanor made an effort to talk to her in a normal manner, asking her about her job, and if she had settled down in Redford.

Wendy watched, puzzled by her mother's attitude. She was used to entertaining all kinds of people. Why should the visit of a girl from the Youth Fellowship have disturbed her?

And then Eleanor Craig asked, "Where did you live before coming to Redford?"

Jean named the midland town where she had been born, and Eleanor's heart seemed to miss a beat. She knew now there was no mistake, no chance resemblance!

Jean, unaware of the havoc she was causing, went on to explain that her mother had died recently, and that she had felt a change of surroundings necessary.

"I'm sorry," Eleanor murmured sympathetically, her voice seeming to come from a distance. "I hope you'll find happiness here in Redford." And then, abruptly changing the subject, she turned to her daughter. "Wendy, why don't you show Jean the things you have ready for your trousseau, and the design for your wedding dress," she suggested.

Wendy turned to her impatiently. "Oh there's time for all that!" she exclaimed. "The wedding isn't for ages yet."

"You wanted it in June," her mother replied, feeling hurt.

"Not necessarily," there was rebellion in Wendy's voice. "You said it was romantic to be a June bride. But the house won't be ready by then. We probably will postpone it until the end of the summer."

Eleanor could not help thinking that if Wendy were deeply in love with Ralph, she would not talk so glibly of postponing their wedding.

Wendy got to her feet as though the room had become suddenly stifling. "Come on, Jean! Let's have that game," she said.

CHAPTER EIGHT

The next day at both morning and evening services Stephen Thornton made an announcement which caused his congregation to sit up and take notice.

"Most of you will have seen from the advertisement in the local paper that we are holding a series of special meetings," he began. "These have been planned to prepare us for the joint campaign which we and other local churches are planning for later in the year. An effort like this needs a great deal of preparation, and not just organizational. I mean on a personal level, in our own hearts and lives, so that God can use us to reach the unconverted people in Redford."

"Because of this I have begun preparing a series of Bible studies to be held each Wednesday evening, studying the different aspects of revival. Study, however, isn't enough. Prayer is the most effective prerequisite of revival. We mustn't forget that it is the work of God's Holy Spirit, and that we are His channels. Unless our lives live up to His requirements, there can be no blessing. Each Monday evening, therefore, we are going to hold a revival prayer meeting, and I want those of you who are genuinely concerned with seeing a revival in this fellowship, to attend these prayer meetings."

The various members glanced at one another. Some of the older ones were thinking back to old James Thornton's days. A few looked openly offended. The younger ones seemed politely bored.

Henry Bellamy shifted uncomfortably. He had warned young Thornton when he'd come out with this proposal at the deacons' meeting, that he was going too far, but once again he'd been outvoted. Henry certainly had no intention of attending the prayer meetings.

Hubert Craig mentally gave the young minister his support. He and William Ogden had been in favor of Stephen's proposal. It was time that something more than lip service was paid in Blakelock Hill Chapel.

Beside Hubert, Eleanor stirred restlessly. She would come, if only in an attempt to find relief from her constant anxiety.

In front of them, Ralph Bellamy decided to respond to the minister's challenge. Wendy, abstractedly twisting her engagement ring round on her finger, reflected that she would support the meetings, if only to gain Stephen's good opinion.

And in a pew at the back Catherine Williams felt her heart strangely stirred. She would be expected to cover some of these meetings, since they were out of the usual run of things, but she knew also that she wanted to come.

Not quite knowing what to expect, Stephen opened the Chapel on Monday evening. The Ogdens were the first to arrive, closely followed by Mary Wilson. She had tried to persuade Jennifer to come, but the girl had replied that she wasn't going in for religion to that extent! Jean had been frankly uninterested.

Donald Waring appeared, giving Stephen an encouraging smile. The Craigs entered just behind him, Eleanor frowning abstractedly. A few minutes later Wendy and Ralph hurried up the path, and just as the service was about to begin, Catherine Williams slipped quietly into a rear pew. Donald glanced at her in surprise. She was the last person he had expected to attend.

Stephen opened the meeting with a well known hymn and after a Bible reading, led in prayer, inviting others to follow his example. The Ogdens prayed aloud in turn. It was obvious they had been longing for something like this to happen. Hubert Craig and Donald Waring took part. The remainder were silent, but they were deeply conscious of the presence of God.

When it was over, Stephen went to the door to shake hands with them.

"This isn't an official visit," Catherine Williams told him smilingly. "You intend making quite a stir in this town, don't you, Mr. Thornton?"

"With God's help I do," he responded quietly.

Donald overheard their remarks. "Don't you think it could do with stirring up?" he asked the girl reporter.

She turned. "I do. I think you've set something in motion that's going to have far reaching effects, Mr. Thornton." She then said goodnight to the minister as some of the others came up to talk to him.

"May I offer you a lift?" Donald asked, following her out of the building.

"Thanks. I've had rather a hectic day. I only just made that meeting, but I was determined not to miss it."

"Frankly I was amazed when I saw you walk in," the doctor told her as he drove away. "I know you've been coming on Sundays, but a prayer meeting didn't seem up your street."

"You should know by now that I am for anything unconventional," she retorted. "As a matter of fact I'm finding this whole business intriguing. It wouldn't take long for Stephen Thornton to persuade me into his way of thinking. He's so completely sincere." Her voice trailed off, and Donald drove the remainder of the way to her flat in silence, his thoughts confused.

He had fallen in love with Catherine soon after they had met in Redford, but because she had so opposed his Christian faith, he had tried to put her out of his mind. Now, however, thinking over her remarks, he wondered if his prayers for her conversion were in the process of being answered. If so, then perhaps there was a chance they might find happiness together.

And, on the heels of that thought, came the unwelcome speculation that perhaps she was attracted to Stephen. Ruthlessly Donald reminded himself that he had prayed for Catherine's conversion for her own sake, and not so that his love for her might be returned. In a spirit of dedication Donald surrendered his hopes and doubts, his love for Catherine and his whole future to God.

His companion, too, was immersed in her thoughts. As he stopped outside her flat she glanced up apologetically. "Sorry I was so mute! Not like me!"

"It seems that meeting has given us both plenty of food for thought," he replied quietly.

"Yes. Well—good night, Donald," she got out of the car. "Thanks for the lift."

"You're welcome. Good night, Catherine." He drove off refusing to look back.

On the Sunday following the first revival prayer meeting, the usual members attended the services. The large number of curiosity seekers present during the first week or two no longer came.

Stephen was aware of the deeper sense of worship in the Sunday morning service, conscious that in some measure his words were beginning to get through to the people. While preparing for the evening service, he had felt led to give a simple gospel message based on Christ's words to Nicodemus, "Ye must be born again!" What better choice of subject could there be in a place so badly in need of a new beginning?

When he had finished preaching, he felt prompted for the first time to give an appeal. "I'm going to ask any of you who have heard the challenge of Christ, and who wish to enter into this experience of the new birth, to come forward while we sing the closing hymn," he announced.

The people, startled by this departure from routine, rose to sing, and then without hesitation Catherine Williams walked down the aisle. Everyone looked astonished. For a moment she stood alone, and then Anne Ogden went to her side to counsel her. When the service ended, he watched the two of them go into the schoolroom where they could talk and pray quietly, and then, encouraged, he walked down the aisle to say good night to his people.

It was in that moment of triumph that Henry Bellamy came up to him, closely followed by his wife.

"Can't say that I approve of these emotional appeals, Mr. Thornton," he said brusquely. "They rarely bring lasting results." And before Stephen could reply, he left the building.

Rita Bellamy, following him, seemed about to say something to Stephen, then changed her mind, and hurried outside.

Presently Catherine came down the aisle with Mrs. Ogden. Stephen took her outstretched hand. "I'm so glad you made this decision, Miss Williams," he told her. "Remember we're here to help you in any way we can."

"I shall no doubt need help," she admitted. "We didn't get started on a very good footing when you first came here, Mr. Thornton, but from now on you can count on my support—for what it's worth."

"It could be worth a great deal," he smiled.

Donald, who had been waiting for Catherine, came forward to offer her a lift home. She accepted readily, but the young doctor was unable to forget her words to Stephen.

Wendy Craig had also overheard the remarks which Stephen and Catherine had exchanged. Once again she was possessed by jealousy. First of all he had seemed to be interested in Jean

Collins, and now it was the girl reporter. Then she realized how illogical her thoughts were. Stephen could not possibly show any interest in her while she was officially engaged to Ralph! If she wanted to win him back, she would have to break with Ralph completely.

Mentally she placed the two men side by side. Stephen, strong willed and resolute, knowing his own mind, going all out for what he believed in. Ralph, hesitant and diffident, running his life to suit other people. There was no comparison.

When she and Ralph left the building, and he suggested going for a drive, she agreed. The spring twilight was closing in when presently he pulled up on a quiet country road. He slipped his arm around Wendy, and was hurt and puzzled when she drew away.

"Ralph, there's something I must tell you," she blurted out impetuously. "I can't go through with our wedding!"

He stared at her as if she had struck him.

"You don't know what you're saying, Wendy," he stammered at last. "This delay over the house has upset you."

"It hasn't," she replied frankly. "It's given me the time I needed to think things out. If my reaction to the delay has been one of relief, that in itself points to the fact that I'm not happy in our engagement. We're not suited, Ralph, and the sooner we break it off, the better."

There was a stunned silence, then he said resentfully, "We've known each other for years, Wendy. You've had plenty of time in which to decide we're not suited. You've only had second thoughts about me since Stephen Thornton came back!"

"He has nothing to do with it," she said too quickly.

Deeply as she had hurt him, the possibility of losing Wendy stripped Ralph of every atom of pride. She had been an essential part of his life for so long, bolstering him up when he'd had no confidence in himself, that he felt now as if his whole world had fallen apart.

"Don't make a decision like this on an impulse, Wendy," he pleaded. "I can't go on without you. I need you."

"Yes." She refused to allow herself to weaken. "That's the trouble. You need me—like a cripple needs crutches, and I've no desire to be a permanent prop! I mean it, Ralph." She slipped the ring he had given her off her finger, and handed it back to him.

"I don't want it," he said bitterly.

"Please take it," she insisted. "I'm determined to make the position clear to everyone."

Seeing that she would have dropped the ring if he hadn't taken it, Ralph placed it in his pocket, and in silent misery started the car.

When he left her in front of Fairview, and drove back to Hillcrest alone, Ralph's anger was not directed against Wendy, but against Stephen Thornton, the cause of their broken engagement. If only he'd never come back to Redford! Ralph knew that his father had opposed it, and had thought at the time that the old man was being unreasonable. Now he shared his father's resentment against the minister. The impression that Stephen had made upon him during the recent weeks was obliterated, together with the consequent deepening of his spiritual life, as he vowed that he would do no more to help the minister.

Letting himself into the house, he opened the door of the lounge to say good night to his parents, determined not to be drawn into conversation.

Rita sighed as he went upstairs. "Ralph looks upset," she remarked.

Henry didn't answer. He was apparently absorbed in some papers he had brought home from the mill, yet he hadn't turned one of them over in the past half hour.

He had hardly spoken since they had left the Chapel, and Rita wanted to talk to him about the service. She watched him in mounting irritation, and at last exclaimed "Henry! Please put those papers away. You're not really looking at them!"

He glanced up abstractedly. "What's the matter?"

"I want to know what's worrying you," she answered. "Ever since we came out of the Chapel, you've looked as if you were carrying the world on your shoulders. You haven't been yourself for weeks. Can't you tell me what's wrong?"

"Nothing—apart from my ordinary everyday worries," he snapped. "Anyone with my responsibilities has continual anxiety. You should be used to it by now."

"It is Sunday night," she pointed out. "Surely you can forget the mill and your other duties at the weekend. I should have thought tonight's service would have helped you. It made quite an impression on me. I've gone with you to the Chapel all these years because you expected me to. Tonight, for the first time, I realized it could mean something."

Unconsciously she had touched on the very source of his moodiness. He, too, had been deeply stirred by the young minister's words, and his conscience was tormenting him. The worst of it was that there was no way out of his dilemma. He was commited to living with it for the rest of his days—unless, and he shuddered at the mere possibility, he made a clean breast of everything, and lost the good opinion of all those who looked up to him. His mind shied away from the prospect, and he wondered desperately how much longer his health would stand up to the strain he was putting upon it. That attack he'd had after Bill Jennings' visit had scared him badly. He hadn't felt like this before Stephen Thornton had come back to Redford. His thoughts circled wildly, like imprisoned birds beating against the bars of their cage.

And then he saw that there was one way out for him. If Stephen Thornton, with his challenging sermons and powerful prayer meetings, were to leave Redford, Henry could perhaps learn to live with himself again, to ignore the past, as he had done all these years.

"So young Thornton impressed you!" he said aloud. "He impressed me, too, with his foolish impetuousity in trying to hook people into the Kingdom with the bait of an emotional appeal. The days of Hellfire evangelism are over."

"So long as people are hooked, does it matter how?" Rita answered. "If you were in danger of drowning, wouldn't an old fashioned fishing boat be just as welcome a sight as the most modern luxury liner?"

For answer he turned his attention back to his papers. "I've more important things to think about tonight than theological arguments," he told her. "There's no need for you to sit up late as well."

Rita got up and went from the room. He had made it quite obvious that he wanted it to himself.

Left alone Henry leaned forward in his chair, his papers falling unheeded to the hearthrug as he stared into the dying fire, his mind engrossed in the problem of how, without revealing his hand in the matter, he could get Stephen Thornton out of Redford.

CHAPTER NINE

The following day Roy Wilson was whistling as he went about his work at the Wayside Garage.

Bill Jennings, employed there as a pump attendant, came in from the forecourt, a disgruntled expression on his face. "Isn't it coffee time yet?" he asked Roy.

The young man glanced at the clock. "Not for another quarter of an hour," he answered.

Bill watched him morosely. He was already bored with the job. He had never been able to settle to anything. If it were not for the fact that he was sure of an income from Henry Bellamy, he would move on, he thought. He hoped there was no danger of that source running dry. He'd written to the mill manager asking for more money, but had heard nothing.

An impatient hooting sounded from outside.

Roy looked round. "You're wanted, Bill!" he told his colleague. "Better hurry. It's the great man himself!"

Jennings swung round to see Henry Bellamy's large black car drawn up by the pumps. He hurried on to the forecourt.

"Fill her up, please!" Bellamy ordered, and stood behind Jennings as he worked.

"Did you get my letter?" Jennings asked him in an undertone.

"Of course, but you surely don't think I'm going to pay up every time you ask," the mill manager replied quietly.

Jennings shrugged. "Redford could do with a diversion," he mused. "I could give it the sensation of all time, if I talked!"

"I meant that I'm not going to keep on paying you just for your silence," Bellamy stressed. "But we could do business together, if you're interested, and you'd make real money."

Jennings straightened up. "I'm interested," he answered quickly. "What's the deal?"

"We can't talk here. Come to my office in your lunch hour."

Seeing Roy Wilson eyeing them curiously, Bellamy paid for his gas, and drove away.

"I didn't know you two were on such friendly terms," Roy observed when Jennings returned to the garage.

Had Jennings not been so full of his own importance, he would have answered more cautiously. Instead he boasted, "Well, we are. He wants me to go and see him." Then he lapsed into silence, but Roy's curiosity was aroused.

He remembered that his father was interested in Jennings. He had been intrigued by Jennifer's account of the man's visit to Bellamy's office. His father would be eager to hear of this latest development!

At lunch time Bill hurried towards the Albion Mill. He was instructed to go straight up to the manager's office. Bellamy was waiting for him.

"Well?" Jennings seated himself at the opposite side of the desk. "What do you want me to do?"

"I want Stephen Thornton out of Redford," the mill manager replied tensely, his powerful hands clenched on the arms of his chair.

"I'll bet you do!" Jenning observed drily. "And how do you suggest I go about it?"

"I don't want any violence—anything obvious. Remember that!" Bellamy stressed. "Use your eyes and ears. Keep a check on his movements. He's young and inexperienced. Sooner or later he's bound to step out of line and make a slip. However trivial, it will give an opening for criticism, for lack of confidence. You could force this, start rumors that will discredit him."

Jennings grinned. "And what about my fee?"

"On the day he leaves Redford there'll be a substantial sum of money for you," Bellamy told him. "Meanwhile I'll give you a retainer. You're not desperate. You've got a job, and the success of this project depends upon your ability to play the part of an ordinary respectable citizen."

"I get it," Jennings stood up.

Bellamy passed him a bundle of treasury notes, and without another word he left the office. The mill manager went to the window and watched him walk down the street. His whole being revolted against the action he had been forced to take, but there was no one else he could have employed. Only Bill Jennings knew him as he really was—Bill Jennings and—God. The thought came to him unbidden. He tried unsuccessfully to stifle it.

That evening when the Wilsons were having their meal, Roy related the incident that had taken place at the garage.

"I couldn't get over it," he finished. "Bill Jennings and Mr. Bellamy talking together as if they were lifelong buddies."

His father gave a mirthless laugh. "They're not buddies— anything but," he returned. "I'd give a lot to know what it is that Jennings is holding over Henry Bellamy."

"I'll do my best to find out," Roy promised.

"You may be successful," Jim mused. "Be careful, though. He's dangerous."

"I'm glad you realize it!" Mary Wilson exclaimed. "Don't get involved with him, Roy. It's none of our business."

"It's intriguing, Mum, all the same," Jennifer put in, adding, "Mr. Bellamy's only been so nervy and irritable since Mr. Thornton came back here."

"Bill Jennings turned up about the same time," her father reminded her. "Perhaps there's some connection between the two events."

"You're all determined to make a mystery out of it, when there is probably a simple explanation," Mary Wilson intervened. "I daresay Mr. Bellamy's not the only person who's become 'edgy' since Mr. Thornton took over at Blakelock Hill Chapel. His sermons have been very challenging. I believe everyone's conscience has been stirred. I know I've realized how far short of Christ's standard I've fallen," she concluded honestly.

"Hooey!" Roy exclaimed derisively.

But for once Jim Wilson did not reject his wife's theory. "Perhaps you're right, up to a point, Mary," he conceded. "About Bellamy's conscience troubling him, I mean. But there must be more to it than just that or Jennings wouldn't have such a hold over him. Henry Bellamy wouldn't go to pieces just because his conscience had been pricked by a few sermons! No, he's got something to hide, and he's acting as though it's something big enough to ruin him, if it ever leaked out."

Jean Collins stirred her tea in silence, thinking over Mary Wilson's statement. She wasn't interested in Henry Bellamy's guilty secrets. She had a more absorbing mystery on her hands. She was still unsuccessful in her efforts to identify the women in the photograph. Now, Mary Wilson's remarks about many people having a new awareness of their guilt since Stephen Thornton's arrival in Redford, had started her off on a new line of thought. She had only to watch for a middle-aged woman who showed these symptoms, and she might have a valuable clue to the identity of the woman. Of course, she had no proof that she was still in Redford, or even likely to attend the Chapel.

Absorbed in her thoughts, she was unaware of Roy's scrutiny. When they had finished their meal, she wandered out into the garden, blind to the peaceful beauty of the April evening.

Hearing footsteps on the path she swung round to see that Roy had followed her.

"It's a lovely night," he remarked.

"Yes," she agreed briefly.

"How about coming for a spin on my motor bike?"

"No thanks, Roy," she answered quickly.

"You haven't much faith in my driving ability," he grinned. "What about a visit to the cinema, then? It would take your mind off your worries."

"Who said I had any?" she countered.

"It's pretty obvious," he answered. "Feel like telling me all about it, Jean? I'd give a lot to be able to help you."

"There's nothing you can do, Roy, thanks all the same," she told him quietly, reflecting that since his father hadn't been able to help her identify the people on the photograph, then he would hardly be able to do. "Find yourself some nice local girl," she told him.

"I'm not interested in the local girls, only in you," he answered.

"You're wasting your time," she replied, walking away from him.

Roy let her go, deciding that there would be no point in further persistence at this stage. Jean had reckoned without his determination. Somehow he would find out what was troubling her.

CHAPTER TEN

A few days later the morning mail brought a letter addressed to Jean. The envelope was printed, almost as if it had been the work of a child, and it bore a local postmark. Jean slit it open and glanced in growing dismay at the contents. Jennifer and Roy had received letters, and they were engrossed in reading them. Jim Wilson was immersed in the morning paper, but Mary, drinking a hurried cup of tea, saw the dawning horror on Jean's face and asked, "What's the matter, dear? Bad news?"

Jean looked up quickly, instinctively folding the letter away. "No. Just something rather—unexpected," she explained lamely.

Hurriedly she got up from the table. "I must rush," she said. "I've some clothes to sort out that I want to take to the cleaners in my lunch hour."

In the privacy of her room she studied the letter again. She had heard about other people receiving things like this, without ever dreaming that it could happen to herself. Jean was still standing by her window staring at the letter when she heard Jennifer run up to her own room. Mechanically she thrust it into her handbag. Then, so as to make her earlier explanation convincing, she whipped a suit out of her closet, and went out on to the landing, calling to Jennifer that she was ready.

She found it difficult to concentrate upon her work that morning. At lunch time, wanting to be alone with her thoughts, and having her visit to the cleaners as an excuse for hurrying away, she told Jennifer that she would not go across to the canteen.

Leaving the suit at the cleaners, Jean walked slowly along High

51

Street. She wanted to find a quiet spot where she could study the letter again without interruption.

Suddenly she thought of the small park behind Craig's Store. She would go there. None of her office colleagues would venture so far from the mill in their lunch hour.

Except for a few children playing on the swings and merry-go-rounds, the park was deserted. Jean crossed the large square of grass to the bench under the shadow of a lilac tree, and sat down.

Opening her handbag, she took out the letter, unaware of Stephen Thornton's approach, until his shadow fell across her.

"Hello, Miss Collins! Taking advantage of this lovely weather!" he greeted her.

Jean glanced up quickly, instinctively crumpling the notepaper into a ball in her clenched hand.

"Mr. Thornton! I didn't hear you coming!" she exclaimed.

"I often take a short cut through here," he responded, wondering what had upset her.

"I came out here for some peace and quiet," she stated. "I wanted to—think something out, and there's so much noise in the canteen."

"And I've interrupted you!" he said ruefully.

"It doesn't matter." With a hopeless gesture she pushed the letter back into her handbag.

He realized that the problem she had brought with her to the park was still unsolved. "If there's anything at all I can do to help, Miss Collins, I'll be glad," he said quietly. "It's part of my job to listen to people's problems, you know."

Jean hesitated. She was used to keeping her troubles to herself, but suddenly she realized how tired she was of battling with them all alone in her isolated little world.

"It's this!" she began unsteadily, fishing the letter out of her bag, and straightening out the creases. "It came this morning, and I— don't know what to do about it."

He took it and read the few lines it contained.

"No happiness can come to you in this town. Be wise and move on before real trouble comes your way."

The note, like the envelope, was printed in large uneven letters, in an effort to disguise the author's normal handwriting. He turned it over thoughtfully.

"Have you no clue as to the reason for this?" he asked her. "Have you quarreled with anyone in Redford?"

52

"No. I haven't been here long enough to make any enemies—unless," her voice trailed off.

"Yes?" he prompted.

"I'd better begin at the beginning and explain why I came here," she told him. "As I mentioned to you, I lost my mother early this year."

"Yes, I remember," he said.

"I had no one else in that area, and I didn't want to keep the house on alone. We'd been very close. Her health had been poor for years, consequently I'd spent most of my time with her, and lost touch with my young friends. I sold the furniture, and I was going through an old bureau one day, when I found a letter and some papers which gave me quite a shock. They revealed that years ago—when I was only a baby, someone had done me and my—mother a great wrong. There was one clue to this person's identity. An old newspaper photograph of a group of women employed in one of the Redford factories during the war, and a remark in the letter that had been sent to my mother with the picture, leading me to believe that the person in question intended settling down in this locality. I've shown the picture to several people, but none of them was able to recognize the women in it. It isn't very clear, you see. Now," she tapped the anonymous letter, "I'm wondering if she has discovered my presence in the town, and because she doesn't want me to track her down, she's trying to scare me away. It's just a possibility—the only reason I can think of for this. Perhaps—if I can find the writer of this note, I shall come to the end of my search."

Stephen sensed that there were many important details she had left out of the story. But it had obviously cost her a lot, proud and independent as she was, to confide in him at all.

"You could take the letter to the police," he suggested. "They have their own means of tracking these people down. As a rule they're to be pitied; more often than not they turn out to be relatively harmless individuals, with too much time on their hands."

"I don't want to do that—at this stage," she returned. "I want to have the satisfaction of tracking her down myself."

"And—if you succeed?" he questioned, "What will you do?"

She glanced away. Somehow she couldn't look him in the eyes while stating her plan of revenge. "I shall confront her with the wrong she's done," she said haltingly, "find out her motive in

53

taking the action she did. I'm curious to see the kind of woman she is."

"Has she a lot to lose by the truth being brought out into the open?" he asked.

"That depends upon her circumstances and her family—assuming she has one. She'd certainly lose the good opinion of those around her."

"Then," he suggested, "don't you think it would be a better idea to let things lie? You say all this happened over twenty years ago. In spite of the setback which this person caused you, you've made out all right."

"And let her get away with it!" Jean objected indignantly.

"I don't suppose she has got away with it," he pointed out. "She's probably done herself more harm than she's done you. If, as you surmise, she is the writer of this letter, then she's probably scared in case you expose her, and on top of that, tormented by a guilty conscience, the worst punishment of all."

"But—if I keep quiet there'll be no justice served out to her," Jean reasoned.

"There'd be mercy," he reminded her. "If people would learn to return good for evil, kindness for anger, Christ's Kingdom would indeed come on earth."

"You can't expect people to behave like saints! We're only human!" She snapped in exasperation.

"Yes," he answered. "Human beings made in the likeness of God—made for communion with Him, and fallen from that state through pride. What a wonderful fact it is that God remembered mercy along with justice, and didn't treat us as we deserved! Instead He made redemption possible through the sacrifice of His Son on the Cross. If you'll take your grievance to God, He'll remove the sting from the memory, and give you peace and a wholesome purpose in life, instead of this desire to have your own back."

She was silent, his words cutting deeply into her heart. Then she reminded herself that words were his business—that he was used to swaying people by his arguments. Abruptly she looked at her watch. "I must go or I'll be late back at the mill," she told him. "Good-by, Mr. Thornton, and thanks for listening to my troubles."

"That's what I'm here for," he returned. "I'll pray for you,

Miss Collins, and in the meantime, if any more letters come, or if you're worried about anything, don't hesitate to come to me for help."

His words re-echoed in her mind as she walked back to the mill. For the first time since she had come to Redford, she was conscious of a little warmth and happiness filtering into her heart. She knew she owed it to Stephen Thornton, and deliberately she fought against the admission. She didn't want to believe in his sincerity. She had come here with a job to do, and if she were not careful he would talk her out of it.

From her father's office which overlooked the park, Wendy Craig glimpsed Stephen's encounter with Jean. As soon as she saw Jean leave him, Wendy murmured something to her father about slipping out for lunch, and raced for the stairs. Reaching the main doorway of the store, she slowed down and rounded the corner of the building just as Stephen reached it.

"Hello!" she greeted him casually. "I was just coming out for a breath of fresh air."

Stephen responded absently, his mind still occupied with his recent conversation.

"My, you are miles away!" Wendy remarked lightly. "Whatever have you got on your mind?"

"All Redford," he returned with a slight smile.

"You do sound grim! And I've got something to discuss with you, too!"

"Well—go ahead," he replied.

"It may take some time," she warned him. "Where are you going now?"

"Back to my lodgings for lunch."

"Then I'll walk up with you. I've an hour to spare," she stated.

They crossed High Street together, and walked toward Blakelock Hill, unaware that Bill Jennings was following them with a satisfied gleam in his eye. At last the minister had given him the beginnings of something to work on!

"The only chance I seem to have to talk to you is in Chapel after the services," Wendy was saying. "And this matter could hardly be discussed there. I particularly wanted to explain about it before the Youth Fellowship. There might be a—difficult atmosphere. You see, Ralph and I have broken off our engagement!"

Stephen stared at her in amazement. "I'm sorry, Wendy," he

55

said at last. "This has come as a complete surprise to me. You seemed so right for one another, and your wedding was being arranged."

"Everything was arranged! That was the trouble," Wendy retorted defiantly. "Mother organized it all, just as Ralph's father arranges his life for him. He's no mind of his own, and I don't intend being stuck for life with a mere puppet."

"I'd hardly describe him like that," Stephen countered. "Ralph's a fine Christian, and it's obvious that he really loves you. I should think carefully before you make the break final, Wendy. Your respective parents have only been so eager to help you plan your wedding because they're fond of you both and want your happiness."

"If that were true, Mother would have seen I wasn't happy, and accepted my decision," she answered. "Instead of that she's done nothing but nag at me since I gave Ralph his ring back."

Stephen didn't doubt this. He remembered how Eleanor Craig had acted when Wendy, as a child, hadn't conformed to the expected pattern. Now in the set lines of Wendy's face he read the same stubbornness that was one of her mother's strong characteristics. He was out of his depths, feeling that this was a family affair, and wondering why Wendy was so anxious to get him to take sides.

"I suppose you've prayed about your decision," he assumed. "If you're absolutely sure you're following God's plan for your life, then you can afford to ignore the comments of others. But do make sure."

She hesitated. That was one remark to which she could not give a glib rejoinder. Stephen Thornton was not the kind of man you could deceive when it came to the subject of prayer. She felt suddenly uncomfortable as she compared the active reality of his Christian faith with the empty formality of her Christian profession.

"I feel that I've done the right thing," she assured him. "Don't turn against me, Stephen. I thought you'd understand. You used to—in the old days."

"I'm not turning against you, Wendy," he answered as they reached his lodgings. "I don't want you to do anything you'll regret, that's all."

"Well—whatever happens, I'll carry on as usual at the Chapel," she promised. "And now I'd better get back into town."

He hadn't been very encouraging, she thought after they had parted. But then he couldn't be, at this stage. When he saw that her break with Ralph was final, it would be different.

CHAPTER ELEVEN

When Ernie Briggs, the owner of the Wayside Garage, had bought the run-down concern outside Redford, he had sensed its possibilities. Standing on a wide stretch of the road, it was conspicuous and easily accessible to passing motorists. To add to its attractions he had opened a restaurant. This was chiefly patronized by traveling salesmen. But frequently some of the local executives would drive out there. Ralph Bellamy had formed a habit of doing this, sometimes with Wendy, sometimes alone. To Bill Jennings' delight, the very day after he had seen Wendy with the minister, the familiar car pulled up, and Ralph and another young fellow from the mill went into the restaurant.

Ralph looked depressed and Bill knew why. He had heard of the broken engagement. Now was the time for Bill to start his campaign against Stephen Thornton.

He waited until Ralph and his companion were seated. Then he picked up a pair of ladies' gloves left by a customer during the week, and walked toward the restaurant.

Waiting for their meal, Ralph and his friend were evidently discussing the broken engagement. "I'm sorry," the other young man was saying. "It's come as a complete shock to me."

Bill gave a discreet cough.

Ralph looked round. "Yes?" he inquired curtly.

"These gloves, Mr. Bellamy," Bill began, "I wondered if they belonged to Miss Craig. I saw her in town yesterday, and tried to attract her attention, to ask her if she'd lost a pair of gloves but she was talking to the minister, and I didn't like to intrude. I thought you'd recognize them if they belonged to her, and give them back to her."

Ralph barely glanced at the gloves. "If they are Miss Craig's, she'll claim them next time she comes in," he said briefly.

Ralph carried on with his meal abstractedly. So Wendy was already going about with Stephen Thornton! She hasn't wasted any time! All week he had worried about the Youth Fellowship meeting, wondering if Wendy would attend it alone. If they turned up independently everyone would start talking. And they'd hardly be able to act as though things were normal.

Now Ralph was sure that Wendy would go. She would hardly pass up the chance of another hour or two in Stephen's company. He decided that he couldn't face it, and resolved to call on the minister on his way back to the mill and hand in his resignation. He knew he would miss the youth work. The hours he had given to it had been among the happiest of his life, yet there seemed no other course of action open to him.

When they reached Blakelock Hill, Ralph instructed his colleague to take the car on to the mill, while he made his call.

Anne Ogden answered the door. "Yes, Mr. Bellamy, Mr. Thornton's in," she answered when Ralph asked to see the minister.

She led the way to the small front room which had been given over to Stephen, and announced his caller.

The minister looked up from the table, where his Bible and some reference books and notes were spread out.

He did well to be so piously engaged in his vocation, when he'd just stolen another man's girl, Ralph thought contemptuously.

"Hello, Ralph. Come and sit down," Stephen greeted him.

"I prefer to stand, thanks, Mr. Thornton," Ralph replied stiffly. "I won't take up much of your time. I can see you're busy," he finished sarcastically.

Stephen was puzzled by his hostility.

"I just wanted to tell you I won't be at the Youth Fellowship tonight, or ever again," Ralph stated. "I'm resigning."

There was a brief silence, and Stephen said quietly, "I'm sorry, Ralph. You've done a great work among those youngsters, and they all think highly of you. It's a serious step to take."

"I've thought it all over well. I'm resigning from Chapel membership, too," he declared. "There's too much hypocrisy in the place."

The old weather-beaten argument! Stephen sighed. Obviously this was a direct result of Wendy's treatment of Ralph. He felt that he could perhaps have helped the young man more, had he been able to come out into the open and tell Ralph he knew what had upset him. But Wendy had spoken to him in confidence, and unless Ralph mentioned the matter, he could hardly do so.

With an inward prayer for wisdom, he said quietly, "I think all of us at some time come to the place where people disappoint us. We have to take our example from Christ, not from other Christians. Pray about this decision, Ralph, and let God deal with whatever difficulties are in the way."

"I've done all the praying I intend to do," Ralph retorted rebelliously. "It hasn't got me anywhere. I won't delay you any longer, Mr. Thornton." Abruptly he made for the door.

Mrs. Craig was Stephen's next visitor. He was shocked by her appearance. She looked as if she hadn't slept for a week. Her face was deathly pale and there were telltale lines of strain that her careful makeup could not hide. She sat down on the chair he pulled forward, clasping her hands together nervously on top of her handbag.

"I've come to see you about Wendy, Stephen—I mean Mr. Thornton," she began. "I'm heartbroken about her. She's ended her engagement to Ralph."

"Then she must have had some doubts about their suitability for one another," Stephen ventured after a brief pause. "And if so, Mrs. Craig, surely it's better that she should break with him now, than have an unhappy marriage."

"That's what Hubert says," she replied. "But I know they could be happy, and I can't bear to stand back and let them spoil things for themselves. Wendy won't listen to me. That's why I've come to you. You two were such good friends in the old days. If you talked to her, I'm sure she'd take notice."

"Naturally I'll do everything I can to help both Wendy and Ralph," he assured her. "But the most important issue, Mrs. Craig, is to pray that God's will shall be accomplished in Wendy's life."

When she had left he had the feeling that his words hadn't got through to her. Finding further work impossible, and realizing he would have to clear his mind in order to fit himself to take Ralph's place at the Youth Fellowship that night, he decided to go for a walk.

He turned on the road that wound above the valley, bracing himself against the wind that swept down from the moors, remembering the many times as a boy he had brought his youthful problems to God in these hills.

Presently a car overtook him and pulled up. Donald Waring looked out. "Can I give you a lift?" he called.

"No thanks," Stephen replied. "I came out for some fresh air and exercise, and to try to get things into perspective."

Getting out of his car Donald came to stand beside Stephen against the low stone wall bordering the road. "I gather you've had a trying day!" he observed.

Stephen nodded his head. "Last Sunday I felt as if I was beginning to get through to the people. And now—everything's gone wrong."

"Didn't you expect that?" Donald countered. "You've been praying and working for revival at all costs," he deliberately quoted Stephen's words. "When you set out to attack Satan's kingdom you must be prepared for opposition! He won't let go his hold on people easily."

Stephen was silent, acknowledging the truth of the doctor's words, and rebuking himself that they'd had to be said. As he looked down upon the clustering rooftops of Redford, he was conscious of a great longing to lift these people out of their narrow rut, and place them on the higher spiritual plain where every true child of God should dwell.

Donald, following the track of his thoughts, placed an encouraging hand on his shoulder.

Stephen glanced at him in gratitude. "Thanks," he said quietly.

He left Donald to continue his drive out to a patient on a distant farm, and retraced his steps into the town, feeling strengthened to face the difficulties ahead.

CHAPTER TWELVE

Prepared as he was for opposition, Stephen was baffled by the form it took. He could have tackled anything that came out into the open, but nothing concrete happened. Instead he found himself up against a growing coldness and hostility. The members listened to his sermons indifferently, carrying out their duties from a sense of obligation.

Donald was his chief standby. He and the Ogdens, Hubert Craig and Mary Wilson regularly supported the revival prayer meeting which Stephen doggedly continued to hold.

There was one encouraging factor at this time, and that was the evident reality of Catherine Williams' conversion. She supported the work loyally, and Stephen felt that if there were no further visible results of his endeavors in Redford, at least he'd had the joy of winning one person into the Kingdom.

Jean Collins continued to attend the Sunday services along with Jennifer Wilson. Stephen gathered that she had not received any more anonymous letters, for she never referred to the subject, but he sensed she was still pursuing the project that had brought her to Redford. Sometimes he would see her glance around the Chapel, as though wondering whether the person she was seeking was present. That was a disturbing possibility, and another factor that troubled him.

Another cause of disappointment was the falling off in the numbers attending the Youth Fellowship following Ralph's resignation. A number of the boys had left immediately, out of sympathy for Ralph. When the news of his broken engagement had leaked out, the young people had taken sides. Some of the girls felt that Wendy had treated him badly, and stayed away because they were disillusioned in her.

There was no one to take Ralph's place. He had possessed a unique flare for the work, and although Stephen didn't spare himself in his efforts to continue with it, the results were discouraging. The youngsters treated him as though he had personally wronged Ralph. They had idolized him, and now they censured the minister.

Wendy carried on with her part of the work, never missing a service, and Stephen felt that she was throwing herself so wholeheartedly into Chapel affairs in order to escape from the difficult atmosphere at Fairview. He was grateful for her help, and Wendy was inwardly elated, feeling that her hopes were nearer to being fulfilled than at any time since Stephen had returned to Redford.

Walking back to his lodgings one day after some visiting, Stephen took a short cut through the park behind Craig's store. It was a sunny afternoon and the swings and merry-go-rounds were filled with noisy youngsters. The seats placed around the park, close to the high hedge which bordered the path, were occupied by young mothers and a few older people. Stephen was hurrying along this path when he heard his name mentioned.

"Of course, it's only to be expected," a woman was saying scornfully. "He is John Thornton's son! There must be bad blood there."

"He's also James Thornton's grandson," an older voice interjected.

"One wouldn't think so from the present state of affairs," the first speaker answered acidly.

Stephen walked on quietly, thankful that the hedge hid him from their view. He knew that ministers came in for heavy criticism, and that in the light of his grandfather's and his father's contrasting records in the town, he would be more liable to it than anyone else, but he was at a loss to know what he was supposed to have done wrong.

Every Wednesday afternoon it was Stephen's custom to visit an elderly man who lived alone in a cottage opposite the Wayside Garage. He had kept to a strict routine with his visiting, so that the people would be able to rely upon him, and not feel neglected. Following this call he invariably caught the bus out to Brentwood, where an elderly lady had gone to live with her married daughter.

Wendy had made herself familiar with his routine. As Wednesday was early closing day at the store she was free, and one oppressive afternoon at the beginning of June, she decided that it was time their relationship took on a more personal note.

She drove out to the Wayside Garage to have her car filled up with gas, timing her visit so that she was leaving just as Stephen came out of the cottage opposite in time to catch the Brentwood bus.

She drew up beside him. "I'm going through Brentwood. If you're going to see old Mrs. Parkes, you may as well have a lift," she told him. "It looks as if there's a storm brewing."

"Thanks, Wendy," he responded abstractedly, his mind still on the visit he had just paid. Immersed in these thoughts, he got into the car beside Wendy, tossing his raincoat into the back seat.

They drove in silence for a while, and at last Wendy challenged him, "Why are you looking so gloomy? You haven't said a single word yet."

"I'm sorry," he apologized. "I was thinking about some of the problems of the people in Redford."

"Don't you ever take a day off?" she asked in exasperation.

"No," he admitted. "I don't think I do."

"Well, it's time you did," she countered. "Everyone needs some relaxation. You weren't so serious in the old days. We used to have such fun together. Perhaps—if I took you in hand, you'd learn to enjoy your leisure again. If you like I'll wait while you call on Mrs. Parkes, and then we'll go for a drive. The change will do you good." The expression in her eyes, the warmth of her smile, rang a warning bell in Stephen's mind.

Surely Wendy wasn't trying to revive their teenage romance? He had never dreamed of the possibility. To him it was nothing more than a closed chapter of pleasant memories. Yet she was always referring to the old days! The thought opened up a disturbing avenue in front of him. Had other people felt that he and Wendy were becoming too close immediately after she had broken off her engagement to Ralph? He had been so grateful for her help in his depleted work, that he hadn't thought how the situation might appear to those who are always ready to read an ulterior motive into the actions of others.

The snatch of conversation he had overheard in the park returned to him, and began to make sense. He knew he had given no real cause for gossip, that apart from this occasion and the day when he had met Wendy near the store, they had never been alone together. But would other people believe that?

He would have to be more on his guard in the future, he decided, feeling thankful that no one had seen him get into the car. He resolved that when they reached Mrs. Parkes' home, Wendy could carry on with her afternoon drive alone! Meanwhile he would have to put her straight.

"In the days you're speaking of," he reminded her, "we were little more than children. Things are different now."

"I haven't changed," Wendy told him, her lips trembling as she recognized the coldness in his tone. "What are you trying to tell me—" she was determined to make an issue of it now, "that you have?"

Embarrassed, he tried to simplify the situation. "I still think of you as a good friend."

"And I've given up Ralph—because of you!" her voice shook with hurt pride and anger.

Her declaration so startled him, and she was so bitterly disappointed with the way the conversation had ended, that their attention was momentarily taken away from the road. Neither of them noticed a dog trotting along on the footpath at its owner's heels. Suddenly it darted away from him in swift pursuit of a cat that had jumped over a garden wall on the opposite side of the road. Wendy screamed and lost control of the wheel; the car swerved and Stephen flung his arm protectingly around her and tried to correct the steering, but the vehicle skidded, avoided the dog, and crashed into a lamp standard.

For a moment or so after the shattering impact everything was black. Then Stephen opened his eyes and moved cautiously. He realized he must have struck his head against the windshield, but apart from that he was unhurt. In swift concern he looked at Wendy. She was slumped against him, white and unconscious, a trickle of blood running down her face from an ugly gash on her temple. Easing her back against the seat, he tried to wrench the door handle open so that he could get help. But the impact of the crash had jammed the door.

The dog's owner, panic stricken at the results of his carelessness in not having the animal on a leash, tried to force the door. Another motorist stopped to help. In next to no time a small crowd had formed, and Stephen was released from the car.

Someone had telephoned for the ambulance and the police, and both appeared simultaneously. Stephen made a brief statement to the police, and then traveled in the ambulance with Wendy to Redford Hospital.

He was so shocked by what had happened, that it was not until he sat waiting for the doctor's report on Wendy that he realized the various implications the incident was likely to have upon his work.

He had insisted upon telephoning Wendy's father himself with news of the accident and was in the waiting room when Hubert Craig and his wife were shown in. Immediately he went up to them.

"I'm terribly sorry about this," he began, but before he could get any further, Wendy's mother turned on him.

"So this is how you repay my trust!" she stormed. "I came to tell you how upset I was about the break between Wendy and Ralph, and you promised to help them, while all the time you were the one who came between them! What right had you to be riding about in the car with her?"

"It wasn't like that, Mrs. Craig," he answered quietly. "Our meeting was quite coincidental. I was visiting over at Brentwood, and Wendy offered me a lift."

"A likely story!" she replied scornfully. "I'm sorry you came back! Nothing has been the same since."

Stephen saw that she was past listening to reason, and withdrew from the room. Outside in the corridor he paced up and down, anxiety about Wendy alternating with the natural distress caused by her mother's accusations. Too late he realized his mistake in accepting the lift. If he hadn't the accident would never have happened. It was understandable that her mother should be terribly upset, but he knew that she would not be by herself in believing the worst of him. There wasn't a thing he could do about it. He could never disclose the nature of their conversation. He blamed himself for having been so slow to recognize which way Wendy's mind had been working.

Desperately he prayed for guidance but there seemed no response. He felt that he had brought disgrace upon the work that was so dear to him by his lack of foresight, and his consequent sense of guilt clouded his communion with God.

At last a nurse came to him. "Miss Craig has been taken up to the ward," she said. "She has recovered consciousness, but the doctor doesn't think it wise to allow anyone other than her parents to see her at present."

"Is she badly hurt?" Stephen asked anxiously.

"She has a broken leg, but apart from that and the cut on her forehead, she's just badly bruised and shaken. It could have been much worse," she finished, trying to console him.

It could, of course, but it was still bad enough, Stephen reflected. Since he was not to be allowed to see Wendy, there was no point in waiting for her parents, and further upsetting Mrs. Craig.

As he made his way up Blakelock Hill, he remembered the Wednesday evening Bible Study. Everyone would be wondering why he hadn't turned up! But the Chapel looked deserted, and glancing at his watch he saw that it was past the normal time for the meeting to finish.

The Ogdens were waiting for him, obviously very anxious. As soon as she saw him, Anne went into the kitchen to make some tea. William drew up a chair for him, and Stephen sat down thankfully, aware that shock was still causing his legs to tremble.

The storm that had been threatening all day broke at last. Feeling that it was nothing compared to the storm which was threatening to break around him, Stephen told the Ogdens about the accident.

"We knew there was something seriously wrong when you didn't come back in time to take the meeting," Anne said.

"I substituted as well as I could for you," William assured him. "We must be thankful the lass wasn't hurt even worse." But in the glance he and his wife exchanged there was concern. They knew Redford, and the issue the townsfolk were likely to make out of this.

"If I were you I'd go and have a rest," William advised him kindly. "You look all in."

Stephen knew, however, that he would not be able to rest. "I'll go and call the hospital," he told them.

Without troubling to get his raincoat, he hurried out of the house to the phone box at the corner of High Street. When he enquired for the latest report on Wendy, he was informed that she was as comfortable as possible. There was nothing more he could do that night, yet he could not bring himself to go back to his lodgings. Suddenly he thought of Donald Waring. He felt in need of the doctor's calm common sense.

Donald's face was grim, however, when he admitted Stephen and glanced at his dripping wet clothes.

"You look half drowned!" he exclaimed. "Come up to the fire and dry out."

Stephen followed him into the lounge, and began to explain the reason for his call. But Donald cut him short.

"I know all about it," he stated. "I've just returned from Fairview. Mrs. Craig was in such a state when they got home from the hospital, that her husband called me in."

"She told you I was out with Wendy in the car when the accident happened?" Stephen asked.

"Yes. I gather she gave you a piece of her mind. I shouldn't worry unduly. When people are in a state of shock, sometimes their minds will shy away from the main source of worry, in this case Wendy's injuries, and fasten on some less important detail—such as your presence in the car."

"But you—" Stephen had to frame the question, "you don't believe I deliberately came between Wendy and Ralph?"

"Of course not!" Donald affirmed.

"Thanks," Stephen responded shakily. "I don't suppose many others will be so generous."

"We can only commit the whole situation to God," Donald reminded him.

CHAPTER THIRTEEN

Stephen's first task the next morning was to telephone the hospital for the latest news of Wendy. He was told briefly that her condition was satisfactory, but that she was not seeing anyone that day other than her parents.

When he got back to his lodgings, Anne Ogden greeted him nervously. "Miss Williams from the *Gazette* is here," she stated.

Catherine sat waiting in the small front room. Her hazel eyes were troubled as she looked up at him.

"I suppose this is an official visit," he began grimly.

"I'm afraid so. It's my job," she answered in a subdued voice. "And I—wanted to handle it. If I don't report the accident, someone else will, and perhaps I can make the facts stand up favorably for you."

Stephen gathered from her remarks that different versions of the cause of the accident were already in circulation.

Sitting down opposite her, he told her how Wendy had offered him a lift because of the threatening storm, that they had been talking, and a dog had run out unexpectedly in front of the car.

Catherine took her notes, impressed as always by his sincerity, and thinking how distressed he would be when the current rumors reached his ears.

She had already been informed that he had been in the habit of meeting Wendy secretly outside the town. It was also being reported that Wendy had been driving with Stephen's arm around her, and that had been one of the contributing causes of the accident.

She got up at last, apologizing for having had to make the call. He walked to the front door with her, and she took his hand in

71

parting and said firmly, "You know I'm on your side, don't you?"

He inclined his head, and watched her walk down the path.

His next caller was a policeman who wanted a detailed statement. And so the distressing day wore on.

Somehow he forced himself to concentrate on the preparation of the evening program for the Youth Fellowship. He reached the Chapel in good time, but at eight-thirty he had to admit that no one else was coming, that the few who had remained loyal after Ralph's resignation, had now decided to boycott the meeting, probably because they were blaming him for Wendy's accident.

He locked up the building at last, and even though it was raining he decided to call on Mr. and Mrs. Craig. They would be home from the hospital and he would find out exactly how Wendy was.

As he was walking up the tree-bordered drive Wendy's poodle flew out at him from the bushes and nipped his ankle.

Hearing the dog barking, Hubert Craig opened the front door and called him off. He made no attempt to invite Stephen into the house, however.

"My wife is still very upset," he told the minister. "I don't think it would be advisable for you to see her, Mr. Thornton.

"I wanted some news of Wendy," Stephen replied. "I understood you were the only visitors she was allowed today."

"She's still badly shocked," Hubert Craig answered slowly, "and, as a matter of fact, has instructed me to ask you not to go in to see her." He saw the minister's stunned expression, and went on, "In view of all that's happened, I feel you'll understand if I hand in my resignation."

He backed into the house and closed the door, leaving Stephen alone on the steps. He sensed that Eleanor Craig had put a great deal of pressure to bear upon her husband. Despondently he retraced his steps towards Redford.

Reaching the top of the hill overlooking the town, Stephen drew level with Henry Bellamy's house. He had thought about Ralph often during the past twenty-four hours. The young man would obviously be upset by Wendy's accident, and no doubt would be blaming him. Stephen recalled Ralph's scornful attitude the day he had resigned. He could understand it now, in the light of Wendy's confession. But no matter how difficult the task proved to be, he felt it was his duty to call on Ralph.

Rita Bellamy opened the door. Her delicately pencilled eyebrows arched in surprise. "Mr. Thornton! We didn't expect you!" she said coldly.

"I wanted a word with Ralph," he explained.

"Well—he's in," she replied hesitantly, "but I don't know whether he'll see you. He's awfully upset about Wendy."

"That's why I felt I had to see him," Stephen answered.

Remembering the rumors that had been going around all day, Rita was puzzled. She would have thought that her stepson was the last person the minister would want to see. She was pretty sure of the kind of reception he would get from Ralph! Thankful that her husband was out at a Council meeting, Rita dubiously admitted Stephen into the hall, and went to the foot of the stairs to call Ralph down.

As soon as he saw Stephen the angry color flooded his face. "I've nothing to say to you, Mr. Thornton," he said stiffly. "And I can't imagine you've anything worth saying to me."

"I came to ask you to let me explain this whole thing," Stephen said. "There is no truth in the stories that are going around. I've had every sympathy with you since you and Wendy split up."

"You've acted as though you had!" Ralph answered scornfully. "You were in the car with her. If it hadn't been for the accident, no one need have been any the wiser. We don't know how long it's been going on."

"It was a chance meeting. Any other Chapel member could have offered me a lift," Stephen reasoned.

"But it happened to be Wendy!" Ralph retorted. "Well, at least I've got the satisfaction of knowing that if she doesn't want to see me at the hospital, she doesn't want you to visit her either."

"I'm sorry you won't try to see the truth," he said to Ralph. "Believe me I only want to help both of you."

"You haven't been very convincing up to now," Ralph flung back. "Dad was right! You should never have come here."

He had barely got the words out when the front door opened and Henry Bellamy came in. None of them had heard his car turn into the drive. He had overheard his son's last remark with dismay. He hadn't wanted Thornton to know how strongly he'd opposed his appointment. It might set him thinking! His objections to the minister's methods since his arrival were logical, but not the fight he had put up before Stephen had even been given the chance to prove himself.

Henry looked from Ralph's indignant face to the minister's

73

serious one. He had never known his son lose his temper to this extent before, and he was surprised to see the boy's spirit. As for Thornton, he had the look of a man almost beaten. Henry began to feel encouraged. Maybe the day was not far distant when Thornton would leave Redford.

"I seem to have come in at rather an inopportune moment," he remarked.

"No you haven't, Mr. Thornton was just leaving!" Ralph said meaningly.

Stephen made for the door. "I'm very sorry about all this," he told the three of them, "more sorry than I can say."

"So am I," Henry Bellamy took command of the situation. "I've grown up in Blakelock Hill Chapel. I shall be sorry to see my association with it come to an end. But in view of the strong family feeling involved, I can't continue attending." As he spoke he was conscious of an inner sense of release. No longer would he have to listen to those disturbing sermons! The young minister had given him the opportunity of resigning on reasonable grounds.

The three of them watched Stephen walk out into the rainswept darkness. Then Henry Bellamy shrugged and went into the lounge.

Ralph, his anger abating, stood at the foot of the stairs looking miserable.

Rita studied him in concern. "You're still in love with Wendy, aren't you Ralph?" she asked him.

He bent his head, embarrassed by the direct question. From the time he had been introduced to his stepmother, he had done his best to give her the impression that he was completely devoid of all human emotion.

"Then why don't you put up a fight for her?" Rita said spiritedly. "You never get anything worth having in this life without fighting for it. It's the way I got what I wanted."

Ralph was silent, surprised, that Rita expressed feelings he thought he alone had.

He watched as Rita, having imparted her advice, turned into the lounge. Then he went thoughtfully up to his room.

Henry was leaning back in his favorite chair, looking more relaxed than his wife had seen him for some time.

"We'll go to the church on High Street next Sunday," he told her.

"It'll be expected that you attend some place of worship!" she remarked sarcastically.

"Naturally. I've always been in the habit of it," he returned.

"Some good it's done you!" she replied. "Christianity is all about brotherly love and understanding. You don't seem to be showing much to Stephen Thornton. He's in a corner, and could do with the support of an influential man like you, and you walk out on him. I've always been proud of you, Henry. I like a person who goes all out for what they want, but I like a clean fighter. I don't like to see you kick a man who's already down."

"You don't understand all the implications," Henry blustered. "Thornton's cause is lost now. It's policy for us to transfer to another church."

"For you—you mean," she corrected him. "I'm answerable to my own conscience."

"You won't support my action in resigning?" he exclaimed incredulously.

"No. I shall carry on at Blakelock Hill," she stated firmly. "I was beginning to get something out of those services. For the first time I saw Christianity as a practical power. I'm not giving up now."

"But—we can't attend different churches, Rita," he protested. "What will people say?"

"I'm past caring," she declared. "I'm sick and tired of always doing the expected thing just because I'm the wife of Councilman Bellamy! You don't care about my personal feelings, so long as I fill my role here. I'm little more to you than that—ridiculously expensive vase on the sideboard that you bought to impress people!" Her voice shook and she hurried to the door.

"Rita!" He half rose from his chair in amazement at her outburst. "Whatever's got into you?"

But she had already slammed out of the room.

Out on the wet deserted road, Stephen walked back into Redford, his thoughts as black as the stormy night. He remembered the enthusiasm with which he had answered the call to this place, the certainty that it was God's choice, the faith and hope with which he had begun his task. And now he had failed. How foolish he would look to the other ministers in Redford to whom he had proposed a joint evangelical campaign. He could see no other course open to him than to resign.

After he had gone, they would all say that he hadn't been able to help making a mess of things, since he was John Thornton's son. For the first time he was aware of sympathy for his father. He knew now what it felt like to be condemned and looked down on.

His thoughts reverted to his grandfather. The old man had been so happy when, as a boy, Stephen had told him that he intended going into the ministry.

"They have a saying in these parts," he had reminded his grandson, " 'from clogs to clogs in three generations.' In our case it'll be 'from pulpit to pulpit.' " And Stephen had failed him!

It was then that the memory of his grandfather began to cut through his despondency. James Thornton had been a fighter. He had had more than one skirmish in his ministry in Redford, but he hadn't let it stop him from carrying on. One of his favorite texts had been from Luke's gospel, "No man, having put his hand to the plough, and looking back, is fit for the kingdom of God". Stephen admitted that he had made mistakes, but then what human being doesn't? He had come to this difficult place at God's call, and therefore it was his duty to stay on and fight until he received instructions to leave. He realized that if he quit now, the sense of this defeat would be with him for the rest of his life.

The plough was God's, and so was the ground—this stony ground which he had tried to break up in order to sow the seed of God's Word, and reap a harvest of souls. He was only God's workman, a laborer to obey orders. It wasn't up to him to say when the day was finished. There would be no more looking back!

Engrossed in his thoughts, Stephen turned on to High Street. It seemed deserted. The sudden heavy downpour must have cleared the town center. And then Stephen realized that he was not alone. Jean Collins, wearing a gaily colored raincoat, was slipping a letter into the box outside the Post Office.

"What weather!" she exclaimed smilingly, and eyeing the soaking wet shoulders of his jacket she exclaimed in concern, "and you were caught unprepared!"

For the first time Stephen became aware of how wet he was. "I've been out for a long while," he explained. "I seem to have mislaid my raincoat." He'd had too much on his mind to be bothered looking for it before he'd left his lodgings. He wondered whether the rumors going around the town had caused Jean and Jennifer to stay away from the Youth Fellowship tonight.

And then, almost as if she had read his thoughts, Jean said, "I came out to mail a letter and get a breath of air. I've been keeping Jennifer company. She's off work with a bad throat."

"I see!" He was relieved. He hadn't wanted Jean to think badly of him. "Did you take any action about that anonymous letter?" he asked her as they walked along together.

"No. I decided to keep quiet about it. I was beginning to feel the whole thing had died a natural death—and then yesterday I received a similar one."

"I'm sorry," he said in a troubled voice.

"I was going to tell you," she said, "and then I heard about the crash. I thought you'd enough problems without being saddled with mine." She glanced at him diffidently, not sure whether he would want her to mention the accident, and yet wanting to make him understand that the rumors had made no difference in her opinion of him. A few weeks ago she would have used them to bolster her cynicism. Now she no longer used it as a weapon to fight her deepening awareness of his sincerity.

"My work must still go on," he answered, and she was satisfied. She knew then that he wasn't beaten, and she tried to encourage him.

"I can't understand these people being so quick to criticize when you've begun to get good results."

"I can only pray about it," he replied simply, "and leave the results in God's Hands."

His words made her suddenly ashamed of the motive that had brought her to Redford. Jean was convinced that the person she was seeking and the writer of the anonymous letters was the same individual. Yet something seemed to be holding her back from making further efforts to track the woman down.

"And what are you going to do about this second letter?" Stephen asked as they approached their respective lodgings.

"I don't know—yet," she answered.

Her tone told him that a lot of the old bitterness had gone. He was thankful for that, and assured her that he would do anything he could to help.

"You've helped me already, Mr. Thornton," she responded, "just by being the same—after all that's happened."

Her words were a gleam of encouragement at the end of a dark day, a proof that he was still capable of serving God in this place, an assurance that he was right in staying on.

CHAPTER FOURTEEN

On Sunday afternoon Jean decided to visit Wendy in the hospital. She brought some fruit and a few magazines, and reached the waiting room to find Mr. and Mrs. Craig already there.

"How nice of you to come! It'll be a change for Wendy to have someone of her own age to talk to," Hubert Craig greeted her.

Eleanor merely nodded stiffly.

Wendy looked surprised when she saw Jean approaching. The girl was the last person she had expected to visit her. She took the gifts gratefully and asked, "What's happening in the town?"

Jean tried to play down the outside situation. She'd heard that Wendy didn't want Stephen Thornton to visit her. People were drawing various conclusions from this, but Jean thought that she knew what was really behind it. Wendy had obviously been attracted to the minister. Perhaps he had discouraged her, and hurt pride was at the root of her attitude.

"Did you go to the Chapel this morning?" Wendy probed.

"Yes," Jean answered, thinking of the pathetically small group of people who had been there.

"When's Mr. Thornton leaving?" Wendy pursued.

"Leaving!" Jean raised her eyebrows. "I hadn't heard that he was!"

"But—Mum and Dad have left, and so has Mr. Bellamy, and quite a few others who helped to run it. He can't carry on without them."

"That remains to be seen!" Jean responded drily.

In relief she saw that Mr. and Mrs. Craig were approaching. Far from feeling sorry for Wendy now, she was conscious of an inner longing to shake her, since she was apparently so anxious to hear of the total collapse of Stephen Thornton's work.

"I must go now. Your parents want some time with you," she said.

"Good-by," Wendy responded abstractedly, noticing her mother's tense expression as she looked at Jean. She recalled the strange effect the girl's appearance at Fairview had produced. What was it about Jean that so upset her mother?

This and the train of thought set in motion by Jean's statement that Stephen Thornton had voiced no intention of resigning, occupied Wendy's mind during the remainder of the visiting hour, so that she only responded half-heartedly to her parents' remarks.

She was relieved when they had gone and she was free to sort out her troubled thoughts. She was depressed by the news that Stephen wasn't leaving Redford. That was all she could hope for now to 'save her face.' She could not bear to meet him after she had so foolishly humiliated herself.

Desperately she began to take stock of the situation. Stephen would play no part in her future, and when she was better there would be no Youth Fellowship, no social life connected with the Chapel to occupy her. She had given Ralph up, and she didn't want him back on the old terms—even if he would have her. The future seemed terrifyingly blank; her life appeared to be totally lacking in purpose. Tears of self-pity welled up in her eyes, and she buried her face in the pillow.

Jean Collins was not Wendy's only unexpected visitor. Catherine Williams, who had spent the intervening days hotly defending Stephen, was instructed by Ted Ellis to try to get a statement from Wendy Craig about the accident.

She went to the hospital on Monday afternoon, sure of finding Wendy alone since her discreet enquiries had unearthed the facts that Eleanor Craig was laid up with a migraine headache, and her husband had gone to the city on business.

Wendy, by this time very bored, greeted Catherine enthusiastically, at the same time bearing in mind the fact that she was, above everything else, a reporter.

"It was nice of you to come," she said.

"Thought I'd see how you were feeling," Catherine began casually. "It's hard on you being fastened up in here—all because a man was careless and let his dog run loose on the road."

"So you know how it happened!" Wendy stated cautiously.

"Oh yes. It's all over town. The dog owner admitted that the animal dived across right in front of you."

"That was all he said?" Wendy insisted. She had wondered whether it had been obvious to the man, who had been walking towards them, that they were arguing, that she was not watching the road.

"Not altogether," Catherine admitted. She explained that the man had said something about Wendy driving with Stephen's arm around her. "But I'm sure an experienced driver like you wouldn't think of driving under those conditions," Catherine assumed. "It's a common cause of accidents, and I don't believe Mr. Thornton would subject you to such a risk. I think the dog owner was confused. It's so easy in a moment of panic to forget the exact sequence of events. To me it seems far more feasible that when the dog ran in front of the car, you lost your nerve, Mr. Thornton leaned across to take control of the steering wheel, and when he saw the crash was inevitable, tried to protect you from the worst of the impact."

Catherine had put forward this theory to everyone with whom she had discussed the accident. It seemed the most reasonable explanation, and tallied with what she knew of Stephen. If Wendy confirmed it, so much the better for him. "Wasn't that what happened?" she asked the girl hopefully.

Wendy lay back in momentary silence, remembering the feel of Stephen's arms about her in that moment before they had crashed. She would never be in his arms again. He hadn't wanted her to be there. He had acted merely out of a sense of protection, just as Catherine had surmised. Stung by the humiliation of these facts, Wendy's mouth set obstinately. Stephen had hurt her, and all she wanted now was to hurt him in return. She could best do that by refusing to admit the truth of Catherine's conjecture. The more people talked the sooner he'd be likely to leave Redford. Let the town think what it would of him!

"I can't remember properly," she said, stifling a yawn.

"That's a pity," Catherine observed curtly. "You'd save Mr. Thornton a great deal of trouble if you could confirm my theory. He's being held responsible by some people."

"I'm dreadfully tired," Wendy sighed wearily.

"All right. I'll go and you can rest. But if I were you," Catherine couldn't resist adding, "I'd rest better when I'd made sure that I wasn't the cause of a man's work being ruined."

She left and Wendy lay still trying to close her mind against that final accusation. Why couldn't they leave her alone? As if she hadn't been through enough! She looked around and caught sight of the dark red roses which Ralph had sent in as soon as he had heard of her accident, even though she had refused to let him come in to see her. With silent eloquence they seemed to plead that he still loved her. In a way she felt almost as sorry for him as she did for herself. They were both victims of circumstances, forced into molds for which they had not been made. Whatever the future held for her, Wendy decided, it was going to be her future. From now on she was going to make all her own choices.

When the *Gazette* was issued on Thursday, it carried a full report of the accident, strongly exonerating Stephen from blame. He read the account, recognized Catherine's work, and was grateful to her.

He did not know that Ted Ellis had remarked to Catherine when he had first seen her report, "We're not taking sides on this issue, you know! This is rather strongly biased in the minister's favor. You carrying a torch for him?"

Catherine had flushed slightly, refusing to give a direct answer. "You wanted an accurate report?" she had countered.

"You don't quote any statement from the girl!"

"It isn't my fault that she wouldn't give any," Catherine answered, adding, "the shock seems to have impaired her memory."

She was reasonably satisfied with the account that was finally printed, however, and on Thursday went to have lunch at the cafe on High Street which she usually frequented.

She was just settling down at a table when Donald Waring came in. Catherine greeted him with a smile, and he came up to her table. It was a while since they'd met. At one time he'd seemed to enjoy her company, but lately he had appeared to be avoiding her.

"Congratulations on that piece in the paper today," he said when they had ordered their meal. "You've struck quite a blow for Stephen."

"I tried to," she admitted. "Whether the townsfolk will be convinced is debatable. People always seem to prefer to believe the worst."

She was evidently deeply affected by all the gossip, Donald realized. No wonder, when she was in love with Stephen. He supposed that he ought not to find it so difficult to accept the situation. He had seen it coming. Maybe he ought to think seriously of moving away from Redford, but he couldn't leave while Stephen needed his support.

His regard for the minister made the position even more difficult. They had talked about the accident and its repercussions yesterday when Stephen had called at his office. He'd caught a chill as a result of the soaking he'd received the night he had walked back from Fairview in the rain, and he had asked Donald to prescribe something to cure it quickly.

"I can hardly stand up in the pulpit and croak like a frog on Sunday," he had told the doctor. "Even if there are only a handful of people present, they deserve the best I can give them for their loyalty."

Donald had given him a prescription, troubled by his strained, exhausted look.

"This place seems to be breaking you up," he had warned Stephen.

And the minister, remembering Rev. Gardener's similar words when he had first come to Redford, had looked serious for a moment, and then responded characteristically, "It's just a question of which is the tougher—Redford, or I. Sooner or later one of us must break!"

"You're very quiet," Catherine's voice cut into his thoughts.

"I was thinking about—all this unpleasantness and gossip," he replied. "I'm not very impressed with Redford. I think I shall move on."

"Oh!" her voice was subdued. "But you won't leave until all this trouble has blown over—surely? Stephen needs what supporters he has."

"Naturally I'll stay and see it through," he answered stiffly.

Catherine got on with her meal in silence, wondering why he was so touchy all at once.

CHAPTER FIFTEEN

That same Thursday evening Jean Collins and Jennifer Wilson walked home from work together.

"We're late!" Jean observed. "We'll have to hurry if we want to be in time for the Youth Fellowship."

Jennifer wrinkled her nose. "Are we going?" she asked. "I heard no one turned up last week, and we're going to feel awfully silly if we're the only ones there."

"If we got ready quickly," Jean suggested, "we could round up a few of the others on the way."

Jennifer laughed. "I didn't know you were so keen on it! You've often said it was just a night out—nothing more."

"So it was—to begin with," Jean returned, following the younger girl into the house. "But now I feel differently."

Jennifer shrugged. "O.K. We'll go then. There's nothing else to do, and I'm not staying in. Dad's in a foul mood because the television set has had to go in for repair." She spoke the last words in an undertone just before they entered the living room.

Jim Wilson raised a morose face from the evening paper, then turned back to it again. Roy smiled across at Jean.

"There's a good film on at the Regal," he said. "Care to come with me?"

"I'm sorry, Roy. Thanks for the invitation," she answered, "but it's Youth Fellowship night."

"I thought that had closed down," Roy replied. "Can't see why you waste your time there."

His mother, coming in just then with their meal, looked at the two girls approvingly.

"I'm glad to hear you are going," she said. "It's sad the way people allow their loyalty to vary with every bit of adversity."

"The folk who've left have come to their senses," her husband grunted.

Mary did not argue. She merely changed the subject and when the girls had gone out, busied herself in the kitchen.

Roy mooned about the living room generally getting on his father's nerves. "What ails you, lad?" he complained. "Can't you find anything to do? Must you pace up and down like a caged animal just because that girl wouldn't go to the pictures with you?"

"The place seems dead without the TV," Roy excused himself.

"You're telling me!" his father retorted. "The mechanic promised faithfully it would be back today. Wait till they do deliver it! I'll give them a piece of my mind!" Then, seeing that he had read every available paper, and Roy was showing no inclination to go out, Jim thought he may as well wile away the evening with his son. "How are things at the garage?" he asked.

"Fine!" Roy responded enthusiastically. "Ernie Briggs has told me I'm getting a raise next week. That's why I felt like celebrating by taking Jean out."

"Well, there are other fish in the sea," his father pointed out.

"Not like Jean. She's different," Roy answered.

"She's that, all right," was the rejoinder. "Bit of a mystery, too. By the way, did she ever find the woman in that old newspaper photograph?"

Roy looked at him blankly. "What are you talking about?"

"Hasn't she shown it to you?" Jim Wilson went on to tell him of Jean's request, and to describe the old newspaper clipping she had shown him. "I suppose she thought you wouldn't be able to help her since I told her we hadn't been in Redford very long," he finished.

Roy was looking at him with a new interest. "No. But I can think of someone who might!" he exclaimed.

"Who's that?" his father asked.

"Bill Jennings, of course. What he doesn't know about the folk in Redford—past and present—isn't worth knowing."

"Pity I didn't think of him at the time," his father answered. "Why don't you ask Jean to let you take the photograph to the garage tomorrow, so that you can ask him? You might do yourself a good turn. It seemed important to Jean to find this woman."

"I will," Roy made for the door. "I'll walk over to the Chapel to meet her."

He left the house, whistling cheerfully. For weeks he'd tried to think of some way in which he could be of service to Jean—without success. Here was an opportunity.

He hung around on the corner near the Chapel until the small group of young people dispersed. Then he caught sight of Jean and Jennifer.

"Buzz off, Jenn," he told his sister. "I want to talk to Jean."

Grumbling, Jennifer walked away, and Roy repeated the conversation he'd just had with his father.

"If you'll lend me the picture," he finished, deliberately refraining from mentioning Bill Jennings' name, for he didn't want Jean mixed up with the fellow, "I think I can find the identity of these women, and what happened to them after the war."

Jean looked at him in surprise. "It's here in my handbag," she responded. "I often carry it about."

His eagerness to help obliterated for the moment the uneasiness she had experienced lately whenever she had tried to resume her search. She was conscious of a mounting excitement. Was her quest really nearing its end?

When Roy arrived at the garage next morning, however, he discovered that Jennings hadn't come in. He wasn't surprised. The man often took an odd day off, and Roy knew that Ernie Briggs was getting fed up with him. There had been some pilfering going on and Roy guessed that Jennings was responsible. He felt that Mr. Briggs thought so, too, but there had been no real proof.

Roy was sure that before long Jennings would drift out of Redford again. He also wondered why Jennings returned to the town, and the peculiar tie-up between him and Henry Bellamy. He resolved to call at the man's lodgings after he had finished work, and ask him about the photograph.

Jennings had a room in a dingy looking street in the drabbest quarter of Redford. His landlady, an untidy-looking, middle-aged woman, opened the door a fraction, and glared malevolently at Roy.

" 'e's in!" she snapped when he enquired after her lodger. "But 'e won't be much longer if 'e doesn't pay 'is rent."

She flung open a door on the right of the narrow passage. Jennings looked up from the evening paper he was reading. "Hello, Roy! Ernie sent you to track me down!" he queried.

"No. I wanted to ask a favor of you," Roy said, producing the faded newsheet, and spreading it out in front of his companion. "I wonder if you can identify the women on this picture. It's very old and not particularly clear, but I thought it was worth a try. You've always known everyone in Redford!"

Jennings frowned as he looked at the date on the top of the page. "You're going back a bit! What's the idea?" he asked curiously.

"Just a personal interest," Roy answered casually.

"What's it worth?" Jennings asked.

"A word in your favor to Ernie Briggs. He's getting tired of some of your habits, and judging from your landlady's remarks, I don't think you're in a position to retire!"

Jennings scowled, unwilling to give information without being paid for it. But Roy wasn't a bad lad. And there was no telling what he himself might need. He had better oblige his workmate. He bent over the picture, his mind going back to the war years, when he'd worked in Redford—in the factory that had since been destroyed by fire.

His gaze roamed along the row of women workers in overalls. They'd been youngsters in those days. Now in most cases they were married women with grown up families. He chuckled maliciously. It was difficult to believe, looking at them nowadays, that they'd once been like this! He began to name them, first of all by their maiden names, and then by their married ones. A few had since left Redford, but the majority had settled down in the town. Roy scribbled the names under the respective faces.

When they came to the center of the group Jennings' finger halted. "She did all right for herself, Nell Gleaves did!" he exclaimed. "Came here with nothing and soon got herself nicely fixed up."

"What's her married name?" Roy asked.

Smiling wryly Jennings gave him the information. Roy added it to the rest, and when his task was completed, folded the paper away. Thanking Jennings he made for the door.

"Your thanks all I get?" Jennings pursued.

Roy grinned. "Gratitude's something, isn't it? I bet there aren't many folk in this town who'd even give you that! And I don't think you're doing too badly," he finished as, opening the door, he caught sight of the raincoat hanging on the peg. "You seem to have been able to afford a new coat."

He swung the door shut behind him and went whistling down the street.

Jennings stood for a few minutes deep in thought, his scheming mind busily assessing this latest development.

He had stayed away from the garage that day because he had gone to the mill for another talk with Henry Bellamy.

"I've come to collect what's due to me," he had greeted the mill manager breezily. "Stephen Thornton will soon be leaving Redford."

"He hasn't gone yet," Bellamy had stated grimly. "He hasn't even announced his intention of resigning."

"It's only a question of time. He can't carry on indefinitely with only a handful of people attending the services, and all this ill feeling. And the retainer you gave me has run out."

"You're not getting another penny out of me until Thornton actually leaves this town," Bellamy had answered. Jennings had sensed that he was less afraid of him than he had been previously. With the tide of popular feeling running against Stephen, he had seemed more self-confident.

"You owe the present situation to me," Jennings reminded him craftily. "Didn't I set those rumors in motion? Wasn't I the one who first noticed that there was something going on between the minister and Miss Craig; the witness who saw them meet outside town the day of the car smash?"

Bellamy had turned away as though the whole business was too distasteful. Bill had watched him closely, sensing his thoughts, realizing that he felt trapped in his own tangled web of deceit, compelled to use the very situation which had caused his son so much unhappiness, to further his crooked scheme.

At this juncture Ethel Blake had tapped on the door. One of the foremen wanted to see Mr. Bellamy about some urgent matter, and Henry had taken advantage of the opportunity and shown Jennings out.

He had left the mill and wandered back to his lodgings, speculating as to his next move. He had gambled away most of the money Henry Bellamy had paid him. He couldn't afford to hang around Redford much longer. It was only a question of time before Ernie Briggs took action. It was impossible to continue to play this slow diplomatic game. Henry Bellamy had let him down. Well—one way or another he would make Bellamy pay!

CHAPTER SIXTEEN

During that week Stephen had formed the habit of going out for a walk last thing at night. He was finding it difficult to sleep, and almost impossible to concentrate upon his work.

On Friday night, thinking about the Sunday services, he crossed High Street, and turned down one of the quieter roads away from the town center. It was here that he caught sight of a familiar figure a short distance ahead. Ralph Bellamy!

Stephen instinctively quickened his steps, hurrying past a small group of people who were talking. Perhaps now Ralph would be willing to listen to him. He had the key to this whole disturbing situation. If only he could make Ralph believe in him, Stephen reasoned, there was a chance of clearing everything up.

He felt suddenly rebellious at the way in which circumstances shaped themselves against him. Why, when he had only sought to do God's will, had God allowed all these reverses? His thoughts grew black and confused as he pressed forward into the night.

In the early hours of the morning, Anne Ogden was aroused by the persistent ringing of the front doorbell. She turned over sleepily, aware that William must have heard it before her, for he was already struggling into his dressing gown and slippers.

"Who can it be at this hour?" she questioned in alarm, looking at the clock.

"I don't know," he answered.

Anne sat up listening as he went downstairs and slid back the bolt on the front door. Then she stiffened in alarm as she heard him exclaim, "Sergeant Brown! What brings you here at this time of night?"

Without waiting to hear any more, Anne got up, and pulling on her dressing gown, went downstairs. In the hall her husband was facing the policeman.

"I'm sorry to have to trouble you, Mr. Ogden," he was saying, "but I'd like a few words with Mr. Thornton."

William looked at him blankly for a moment, then said, "Very well, Sergeant. Come into the living room. I'll get Mr. Thornton."

Anne went with the policeman while her husband climbed the stairs and knocked on the minister's bedroom door. It was opened immediately. To William's surprise Stephen was fully dressed and his bed had evidently not been slept in. He looked very pale.

"Sergeant Brown wants to see you, Mr. Thornton," William explained. He had the uncanny feeling that this was all a dream.

Stephen looked dazed. "To see me?" he repeated.

William nodded. "He didn't say what it was about."

He turned and led the way downstairs.

Sergeant Brown looked surprised to see the minister fully dressed. "Haven't you been in long, Mr. Thornton?" he asked curiously.

"Well—yes," was the confused answer. "I just—didn't feel ready for sleep. I was sitting up in my room—thinking. What did you want with me, Sergeant?"

The policeman studied him thoughtfully. "Ralph Bellamy was found a short time ago—unconscious, with head injuries," he said tersely.

"Oh no!" The exclamation seemed wrenched from the minister. "Is it very bad? Do you want me to go to him? Is that why you're here"

"He's not likely to die," the policeman replied brusquely. "He's in the hospital, and it will probably be some time before he regains consciousness. Meanwhile I'd like you to explain what your raincoat was doing near the spot where he was found."

"My raincoat!" Stephen repeated.

"Yes. This is yours, I believe." The policeman held out the coat which had been folded over his arm. "There's an opened envelope in one of the pockets addressed to you."

"Yes—it's mine," Stephen confirmed. "But I can't understand how it got there. It's been missing—" his voice trailed away as he looked from the Sergeant's skeptical face to the Ogdens, who were watching him with troubled expressions. Suddenly the reason for the policeman's visit seemed startlingly clear. "You surely don't think I'm responsible for Ralph's injuries?" he demanded hoarsely.

"The couple who found him stated that they saw you hurrying after him a short time before," was the reply.

"I did hurry after Ralph," Stephen admitted. "I wanted to talk to him—to try to clear up the misunderstanding between us. He turned and saw me, and then hurried on faster than ever. I saw there was no point in trying to force him to talk to me—so I gave up the chase and walked through the town."

"And what time did you get back here?"

Stephen passed a hand across his forehead. "I don't remember," he said in confusion. "Can I see Ralph?" he asked.

The Sergeant shook his head. "His people are there, and one of our men is waiting for him to make a statement when he comes round. We shall want to talk to you in the morning, Mr. Thornton, so please see that you're available. I'm sorry I had to disturb you," he apologized again to the Ogdens as he went out.

"You surely don't think I did it!" Stephen greeted William as he came back from seeing the Sergeant out.

The deacon didn't answer him directly. Shaking his head in a dazed fashion he said heavily, "I never dreamed the old Chapel would be the center of scandal and violence."

"Sit down and I'll make some tea," Anne said kindly in the tone she might have used to an erring son.

"No thanks," Stephen felt that the tea would choke him. "I'll go back to my room."

As he went slowly upstairs he could hear them talking.

"It's a mighty queer business," Anne said. "I can't believe the pastor would get involved in a brawl, and yet—he's not been himself this week—tramping the streets at all hours. He never told us his raincoat was missing!"

"He's John Thornton's son!" William responded, as if that explained the whole matter. "We mustn't forget that."

He ought to have remembered it himself, Stephen thought wearily as he flung himself on the bed. It looked as if he would never live it down.

The following afternoon Rita Bellamy watched anxiously for Henry's return from the hospital.

They had both spent an anxious night there waiting for Ralph to regain consciousness—but he hadn't done so, and early this morning Henry had driven her home, insisting that she should rest. She had gone to lie down, but sleep had eluded her, and after Henry had again left for the hospital, she had gotten up.

Her strained nerves felt close to breaking point when she caught sight of Ethel Blake's gaunt figure looming up the drive. Rita knew that her husband's secretary despised her, and she was tempted to pretend that she wasn't in. Then she rebuked herself. After all, it was good of Miss Blake to come.

She went to admit her visitor. "I didn't think you'd be at home, Mrs. Bellamy," Ethel greeted her, the statement sounding like a rebuke. "I was sure you'd be at the hospital, but I had to call just in case you were in, to see if there was any further news about Mr. Ralph."

"He was still unconscious when I left this morning," Rita said, leading her visitor into the lounge. "They told us it might be some time before he came round. My husband has gone back there to wait."

"Oh!" The single word conveyed Miss Blake's disapproval.

Rita felt that she had to get out of the woman's presence. "I was just going to make some tea," she said. "You must have a cup with me." She went into the kitchen and busied herself preparing a tray.

Ethel Blake seemed determined to stay until Henry returned. When he entered the house at last she studied his tired anxious face in concern.

"Is there any better news?" she asked before Rita could get the question out.

"He's recovered consciousness," Henry responded. "I'll take you back this evening," he told his wife.

"Do they know definitely who's done it?" Ethel asked him.

"Ralph can't remember anything clearly. I was only with him a short time," Henry answered.

"Everyone's saying it was the minister," Ethel pursued. "He was seen hurrying after Ralph. People seem to think they quarrelled about Wendy and Mr. Thornton lost his temper. It seems unbelievable, but then —he is John Thornton's son!"

"Yes," Henry replied briefly. "We shall know something soon." He stood up. "If you like I'll run you home in the car, Miss Blake. It was kind of you to come."

It was a polite way of dismissing her, Ethel knew. "Oh no, I wouldn't dream of putting you to that trouble," she demurred. "You need a rest before you return to the hospital, and I have some shopping to do on the way home."

Rita said good-by to her abstractedly, and when Henry came

94

back into the lounge after seeing her out, she asked him, "You don't really think it was Mr. Thornton, do you?"

He was momentarily silent. "His raincoat was found nearby," he reminded her. "And they did have a quarrel that night when Stephen called here after Wendy's accident—at least Ralph lost his temper. Maybe Ralph tackled him again and they came to blows. From all accounts his injuries could have been inflicted either by a blow struck from behind or as the result of a fall against the curb in some kind of scuffle. His wallet has been found several hundred yards away, too. It was empty!"

"Then that lets the minister out," Rita responded in relief. "Even if they did have a scrap, and Mr. Thornton panicked and left him, which I find impossible to believe, he'd never take Ralph's wallet."

"No. But it's possible that someone else saw Ralph lying there and went through his pockets. It's been done before on the scene of an accident. The police seem to be working on that theory. It all happened in a rough quarter, remember."

He sank back into his chair and closed his eyes. Rita watched him in troubled silence, aware again of the growing distance between them. They should have been able to help one another at a time like this; yet she realized that Henry was miles away, locked in his own private world, from which he had once again shut her out.

In the narrow hospital bed, Ralph lay with his eyes closed against the light. Subdued voices passed in and out of his hearing. The two young nurses changing the empty bed nearby were excited by his admission to their ward under such dramatic circumstances. Unaware that he was now listening to them, they carried on with their conversation.

"Fancy the minister being responsible for young Mr. Bellamy's injuries!" Ralph heard one of them say.

"It's hardly surprising," her companion returned. "Mr. Thornton's only a man, not a saint, and since he and Ralph both wanted the same girl, what can you expect but trouble! Of course this'll finish the minister in Redford—maybe finish him altogether!"

The full implication of the words sank slowly into Ralph's mind. His father had tried to question him about what had actually happened, but then everything had been hazy. The police were waiting for him to make a statement, but as yet he hadn't felt able to do so.

Now, thanks to the conversation he had just overheard, he was beginning to remember. A grim smile played about his lips. He could tell all those who were anxiously awaiting his report anything they wanted to know, and at the same time settle his account with Stephen Thornton once and for all!

CHAPTER SEVENTEEN

For Stephen Saturday· dragged interminably. The police questioned him about his movements the previous night, and he could only repeat his original statement which he knew did not sound very convincing.

In the afternoon he was forcing his thoughts on to the following day's sermons, and wondering whether the effort was worth while, for it seemed likely that he would face an empty Chapel, when Anne Ogden showed Donald Waring in.

Almost the first thing Donald noticed was the envelope which Stephen had addressed to Rev. Gardener, propped up against the clock.

"You're not resigning!" he exclaimed in dismay.

"Not in so many words—although the outcome will be the same," was Stephen's rejoinder. "I've written to Mr. Gardener telling him all that has happened. He'll be bound to come here to sort the whole thing out, and then he'll probably relieve me of my charge. If he doesn't the local folk will demand my resignation."

"But—surely you're going to fight to prove your innocence? Donald objected.

"I can't prove it—even to myself!" was the surprising answer, as Stephen walked over to the window.

"What are you trying to say?" Donald followed him.

"Simply that I can't remember what happened after I started following Ralph," Stephen told him. "I know it must sound crazy, but I distinctly remember hurrying after Ralph, feeling that if I could only make him see the true position, the whole situation might be altered. But he saw me and wouldn't let me catch up with him. I remember feeling very angry, rebellious about the injustice of it all, and—nothing else—until I found myself walking through the streets a good distance from where I'd last seen Ralph. I must have had some kind of a black out. But the question is—what happened during that time? Did I hurt Ralph? I can't be sure I didn't. You don't know what I've gone through today wondering—" His voice trailed off and he sat down wearily.

"Have you ever had a black out before?" Donald questioned him.

"No," Stephen shook his head. "Why?"

"This could have been the result of that knock on the head you got when Wendy Craig's car crashed just over a week ago. It's possible it was a kind of delayed reaction," Donald explained. "The strain you've been under since then could have brought it on."

"That isn't the important issue," Stephen answered bleakly. "The fact is it happened, and I don't know what I did during that time. It's my own fault, I suppose. I was proud and stubborn, believing I could take on a place like Redford and win. I came here to build up God's work, and instead of that I've set it back—just like my father did," the last words were spoken in an undertone. "My grandfather would be ashamed all over again if he could see this day."

"He would if he could hear you talking like that," Donald turned on him. "Think of all you planned to do here! Remember all those early prayer meetings! You can't let all that go to waste. You knew there would be opposition. Don't give up underneath it. Let's pray about it together—pray that in spite of the apparent hopelessness of the situation, revival will still come."

"That's the worst factor of this whole thing," Stephen said quietly. "I can't seem to pray any more. I feel—forsaken." He leaned his head on his hands.

Donald stood for a moment in helpless silence, then he put his hand on the minister's shoulder. "But you're not—no matter what you may feel," he said firmly. "God has promised to be with us in all things. That's an unalterable fact, however shaky your faith may seem just now. Maybe—if I prayed it would help." He knelt down and, just as though he were speaking to a Friend in the same room, he laid the whole complicated affair before God.

When they got to their feet Stephen gripped his hand in gratitude. Then Anne Ogden knocked at the door to say that Miss Williams wished to speak to the minister.

"I suppose you want some comment on all these stories that are going around about the attack on Ralph Bellamy," Stephen said to the girl reporter. "I'm sorry, Catherine, but this time I can't oblige. Perhaps you'll explain, Donald."

The young doctor told Catherine about the temporary black out which had rendered those vital minutes into a confused blur in Stephen's memory.

"You couldn't have done anything like that!" Catherine declared. "It's completely out of character."

"Why don't you come back to the flat and have dinner with me?" Donald suggested to Stephen.

"No thanks," Stephen responded. "I was told to keep myself available, so I'd better stay here. And I must finish my preparation for tomorrow. This could be my last Sunday as a minister here. I want to give of my best, although I don't suppose there'll be many people present to listen."

"We'll be there," Catherine promised loyally. "I'm convinced that your work isn't finished here."

Later, as Donald drove her home, he remarked on her unusual silence.

"I'm worried about Stephen," she told him. "I wouldn't say anything in front of him, but just before I called at his lodgings, I went to the hospital to get the latest bulletin on Ralph. He had just told the police that he remembered having an argument with Stephen. He accused him of being responsible for Wendy's accident, and Stephen went for him. What do you make of it?"

"I think there's a great deal more in this whole business than meets the eye," Donald answered. "Ralph's had it in for Stephen for some time. It would suit his purposes to use this latest development to get rid of him."

"Yes," Catherine replied, the familiar light of battle in her eyes." I think I'll have a talk with Mr. Ralph Bellamy!"

She got out of the car, unaware of the tender expression in Donald's eyes, her whole being focused on fighting this latest of Stephen's causes.

Stephen went into the Chapel on Sunday morning wondering how he was going to get through the next difficult hour. He looked around at the few familiar faces: Catherine and Donald, Anne and William Ogden, who had come, he suspected, more out of loyalty to the old Chapel than to him; Mary Wilson with her daughter, and Jean Collins.

At the back, as though afraid of being identified with the proceedings, were a few youths. Stephen recognized them as belonging to a gang that had occasionally caused trouble in the town. They had probably come out of curiosity, anxious to see in action this parson who went around knocking people out, Stephen reflected grimly. And then he realized that God had even made use of this latest blow in bringing in these young people, who, in the ordinary course of events, would never have attended a service.

That revelation gave him the inspiration he needed, and he spoke with a burning sincerity of the love of God that never changes, though everyone and everything on earth may change. The Eternal Love that is always there behind the storm clouds and the darkness, even when we cannot recognize it in action in our difficult pathway. He spoke to himself as well as to the people present, knowing that the love of God was the only fact he had left to cling to, and aware, with a deepening sense of comfort, that it was sufficient.

When the service ended he hurried down the aisle to speak to the teenage boys. They were practically out through the door by the time he got there, and they answered him in clipped, careless tones. But one of them, a small, thin lad with long hair almost hiding his eyes, looked at Stephen with a newly thoughtful expression that had in it a hint of respect.

"It seems you can punch with words, too, Padre!" he exclaimed as he hurried away after his companions.

Jean was very quiet on the way back to her lodgings, letting Jennifer's incessant chatter slide past her unheeded. During the service she had practically forgotten the subject that had been uppermost in her mind ever since the moment on Friday night when Roy had come home with the names of the people on the old newspaper photograph. At last Jean felt sure she knew the identity of the woman she had been seeking. She had checked over the few facts she had with the information Roy had obtained, and they matched up.

She had stayed awake half of Friday night trying to formulate a plan of action, her relief that her enquiries had at last been successful, dampened by the memory of Stephen Thornton's gentle rebukes. And then on Saturday morning the news of the attack on Ralph Bellamy and the discovery of the minister's raincoat nearby had taken her mind off her own problem.

In her early days in Redford, Jean would have sided with those people who were condemning the minister, but now she found that she believed implicitly in him. This new disaster affected her in a strangely personal way which she could not define.

She was too distressed by the whole bewildering affair to think of stirring up any more trouble. And somehow, after this morning's service, it was impossible for her to go on bearing malice. As Stephen had spoken of the love of God, Jean's restless searching heart had reached out and been met by the seeking love of the Saviour. She knew her life would never be the same again. It was as if a heavy burden had rolled away.

Over the Sunday dinner the conversation turned to the subject of the morning service.

"I suppose you three were the only ones stupid enough to go!" Jim Wilson sneered.

"No, Dad. Art Wilkins and some of his gang were there," Jennifer answered.

"Well—that's the kind of circle young Thornton can expect to move in now," her father replied. "And you'll be getting the same kind of reputation if you keep on attending."

"Oh, come off it, Dad!" Jennifer answered. "You know you don't really think it was Mr. Thornton who knocked Ralph Bellamy out!"

"Why not? He's only human. Just because he wears a dog collar doesn't make him any different from the rest of us."

"There are some things you just know some people couldn't do," Jennifer declared, "no matter how the circumstances make it seem."

"That's true," Jean agreed feelingly. "But there must be some way of proving it to all the doubting Thomases in Redford."

"There was the proof of his raincoat, found where he must have dropped it when he ran away," Jim Wilson reminded them.

"The raincoat!" Jean mused aloud. "Of course! Why didn't I think of it before?"

"Think of what?" Jennifer asked quickly.

"The fact that—someone else could have dropped that raincoat!"

"What do you mean, dear?" Mary Wilson asked her.

"I saw Mr. Thornton a week ago last Thursday night. We walked up High Street together. If you remember it was raining, and he wasn't wearing a raincoat. He said something about having mislaid it."

101

"But that doesn't prove anything," Jim Wilson reiterated. "Perhaps he'd been too worried to look for it. That heavy downpour didn't start until late in the evening. It was probably fine when he set out."

"Yes," Jean agreed dubiously. "But the weather's been stormy ever since, and I haven't seen him wearing a raincoat." She knew it was only a theory, but she clung to it with a stubborn hopefulness. "Maybe I ought to go to the police."

"You're trying to say that Mr. Thornton lost his raincoat sometime before the night you met him, more than a week before this attack on Ralph Bellamy?" Jennifer countered.

Jean nodded.

"Then why hasn't he explained that to the police?" Jim Wilson stated.

"Perhaps he has and they won't believe him!" Jean pushed back her chair. "Maybe—if someone else confirmed it—" she got to her feet. "I'm going down to the station."

"Wait a sec. I'm coming with you!" Jennifer slammed down her empty coffee cup and hurried after her friend.

Roy, who had been listening intently, remained unusually silent. At last, looking thoughtful, he got up and went out of the house.

Half an hour's brisk walking brought Roy to the seedy looking street where Bill Jennings lodged.

His landlady opened the front door a few inches, and scowled at Roy from beneath a formidable array of hair rollers. She obviously remembered his visit on Friday.

"Yer mate's gone!" she told him belligerently. " 'opped it owin' me a month's rent 'e 'as."

"I'm sorry," Roy answered in dismay. Yet he was not surprised by the news. "When did he leave?"

"Must 'ave bin early Saturday mornin'!"

"If I could have a look round his room, maybe I could find a few clues as to where he's gone," Roy suggested.

" 'is kind don't leave no forwardin' address!" she sneered. "All 'e left was a pile of old newspapers."

"Newspapers!" Roy's interest was immediately aroused. "Have you still got them?"

She nodded. "They're still on the table in 'is room. I 'aven't bothered to do it out yet."

"If you'd let me go through them, I might be able to get on Jennings' track," Roy told her.

"Oh, all right," she moved back, opening the door wider. " 'elp yourself. Give me a shout when you've finished."

Roy entered the room, found the pile of papers, and began to turn to the advertisements columns. It was a long shot, but he could not think of any other way of getting a clue as to the man's whereabouts. He had left Redford in a hurry, but he must have given some thought as to his destination. In his financial fix, he would have to go where there was work, and it was just possible that these advertisements would be the lead. At last Roy came across the information he had hoped for. Three advertisements for gas pump attendants had been underlined in pencil. They all notified vacancies in the Moorfield area, a town about fifteen miles away from Redford. Roy picked up the paper and walked to the door.

"I've found what I was looking for," he called to Jennings' landlady. "It might be that he's made for Moorfield. I'll perhaps be able to locate him."

"If you do, remember I want my money," she retorted.

Roy left the house eagerly forming a plan. The week ahead was one of his two annual holiday weeks. He had intended leaving it free to spend just as he felt inclined. No one would question him when he stated that he was going out for a run on his motor bike tomorrow.

He knew he ought to give the information he had, and the theory on which he was working, to the police, but he had no intention of doing so—at this stage. He had been curious about Jennings for too long, intrigued as to the hold the man had possessed over Henry Bellamy. Now he may be in a position to threaten Jennings, just as the scoundrel had threatened others, and find out all he wanted to know.

CHAPTER EIGHTEEN

Wendy Craig picked half-heartedly at the chocolates which her father had brought her, and tried to focus her attention on his remarks.

On this Sunday afternoon visit, Hubert and Eleanor had carefully broken the news of Ralph's injuries to Wendy. She had obviously been shocked and upset.

"Why don't you write a little note to Ralph, telling him how sorry you are about—everything," Eleanor suggested to her daughter. "I'm sure things could still work out all right."

"You still think you'll get the two of us together again, don't you, mother?" Wendy answered. "Things have gone too far for that."

"Don't you feel sorry for Ralph?" her mother persisted.

"Of course I do," Wendy retorted indignantly. "I always have. That's what's been wrong."

Hubert at last managed to get his wife out of the ward without any further mention of Ralph, and Wendy was left alone with her thoughts.

They were not pleasant ones. She was very upset about Ralph's injuries, and conscience stricken now by the harm she had done Stephen Thornton.

She remembered how jealous Ralph had always been. Had he gone for the minister on Friday night, and had Stephen struck out automatically in self-defense, and then panicked? Yet it was difficult to reconcile such an action with what she knew of him.

Wendy turned the problem over in her mind, but she was still no nearer a solution. She slept little that night, and was heavy eyed and listless when one of the nurses handed her a note the next morning.

She split open the envelope, and withdrew the folded sheet of paper. As she did so, she caught sight of the signature— 'Jean Collins'.

"I hope you're feeling much better," Jean had written. "I wanted to come and see you yesterday, but I didn't like to crash in again while your parents were there. I wondered if you knew exactly what has happened since Ralph was found injured on Friday night. You will have heard, I suppose, that Mr. Thornton is being held responsible, and that Ralph has made a statement confirming this. But several of us feel that there is far more to all this than meets the eye. You are the only person who can help to clear up this muddle, for you alone know the true situation involving yourself and Ralph and Stephen. When anything like this happens in a town the size of Redford, everyone takes sides. The work at Blakelock Hill Chapel is being ruined, and I appeal to you to do what you can to clear the matter up. A few words from you could save a man's career. Surely you—as a Christian—cannot willingly allow a fellow believer and the very cause you profess to serve, to suffer because of a misunderstanding."

Four words out of the letter burned themselves into Wendy's mind. "You—as a Christian." She recognized the query beneath Jean's words. Jean, who, on her own admission had never bothered about Christianity before coming to Redford, was searching now to see if there was any depth of sincerity behind the Christian profession of the girl who had led the Youth Fellowship.

Wendy crumpled the letter up and turned her face away from the other occupants of the ward, conscious of an overwhelming sense of humility and defeat. Again she remembered how impressed she had been by the contrast between Stephen's living faith and the empty profession of Christianity which was all she had. But why hadn't it mattered to her in a personal sense, when she'd been brought up to attend Chapel? Bit by bit the answer came. It was because she'd never really come face to face with the challenge of Christ, never seen herself as a sinner needing the salvation He alone could give. She'd thought it was enough just to go to Chapel. But in actual fact she'd only made use of the place, filling up her life with its social activities, not serving out of love and gratitude to God.

Even her dealings with Ralph had their roots in selfishness.

She'd allowed herself to be talked into an engagement with him because he was in a position to give her all the things she wanted in life. As for Stephen, she had imagined that she loved him, but if there had been anything of real love in her heart, she would never have kept silent this past week, and allowed him to be misjudged, and the work which meant everything to him jeopardized. Stephen's return to Redford had been a welcome diversion from the monotony of the engagement to which she should never have consented. It had provided her with the necessary impetus to take some decisive action. That was all!

In fact, Wendy realized miserably, she had never loved anyone other than herself. And now she was left alone with the ruins of her own narrow world all about her. She knew that Jean had spoken the truth in her letter. She held the key to the situation. Whatever she did would effect both Ralph and Stephen. How could she ever be free from this awful responsibility?

In desperation she reached for her handbag and took out the small Bible which she carried but rarely read. She opened it, seeking guidance now with a new sense of need. Some words she had underlined during a Bible Study leapt up in challenge— "the truth shall make you free".

Her face was white and tense. Only by admitting her foolishness, by being prepared to let others see her as she really was, could she find freedom from this nagging sense of guilt. And she wasn't big enough to do it—alone! Bending over the Bible she began to pray sincerely for the help she needed.

That same day Ralph Bellamy had an unexpected visitor, Catherine Williams. He was surprised and flattered when she came up to him. Accustomed for years to accepting the fact that he was of little importance, Ralph was finding this sudden thrust into the limelight unexpectedly pleasant.

"I suppose you want my story," he assumed. "You only just got here in time. I'm being allowed to go home later today."

"I'm glad to hear it," Catherine responded. "I take it that means you're well on the way to recovery from the effects of the— accident," she used the word deliberately.

"Accident," he repeated indignantly. "Don't you mean 'attack'?"

"Do I? You should know! You're the only one who can fill in all the details," Catherine answered casually as she sat down.

"I've already made a statement to the police," he replied.

"So I heard. But I wasn't present. This is for the *Gazette*. I'm sure you want me to have the facts right. It must be important to you to see that the truth is printed."

He glanced away uncomfortably. "You know what happened," he hedged. "It's already gone the rounds of the town. Wendy and I would have been getting married this summer if Thornton hadn't come back and taken her away from me!"

"But he hasn't taken her away from you, has he?" Catherine prodded mercilessly. "She hasn't wanted to see him since the car crash. So you've no longer any reason to be jealous of him. It makes me wonder why this—fight started."

Ralph passed a hand across his forehead. "It's difficult to remember," he said slowly. "You'll have to give me more time, Miss Williams. I wasn't—prepared for your visit, remember."

"I can't see that giving a simple statement of the facts needs preparation," Catherine objected, getting to her feet. "I'll see you again. Mr. Bellamy, Good-by for now," she stressed the last word.

She held out her hand in parting. Ralph took it, and as he did so, she studied both his hands closely. Then she remarked cryptically, "For a man who's supposed to have been in quite a scrap, you're not carrying many bruises! Funny! I noticed the same thing about Mr. Thornton's hands on Saturday."

Ralph watched her walk away, the assured confidence in her step disturbing him.

Later in the day, as his father drove him home, Ralph told him about Catherine's visit.

Henry Bellamy was silent for a time, then he said brusquely, "You must stick to your story. That's all you can do."

The words were in the nature of a command rather than a piece of advice. Ralph had the sudden impression that beneath his grim quiet manner his father was afraid; that Catherine's remarks had upset him.

He was not accustomed to seeing his father show fear. He had imagined he was the only member of the family afflicted with it. It seemed to put them on a common level, and it was quite a novel experience. After the preferential treatment he'd been receiving all weekend, Ralph had not relished the prospect of going back to the grind at Hillcrest and the mill as a mere nonentity—to walk in his father's shadow.

"Stick to your story," Henry Bellamy said again as he turned in at the wide gateway of Hillcrest.

"The story I told the police!" Ralph stated quietly.

"What else?" Henry replied.

It struck Ralph then that his father had been singularly satisfied with the statement he had made to the police. He hadn't asked his son to explain it in any more detail when they had been alone. In fact he'd refrained from discussing it. And that was odd. Very odd!

As Ralph went up the steps he remembered his father's earliest opposition to Stephen Thornton's appointment. It was almost as if the minister's presence in the town had threatened his position in some way. Right from the start Henry Bellamy had been anxious to get rid of Thornton, and he, the despised weak-willed son, had been instrumental in bringing it about, Ralph reflected with satisfaction. Thanks to this fact there was now a reversal of roles. His father depended on him to stand by the statement he had made until Thornton was finished in Redford. For the first time in his life Ralph experienced a sense of power, and it went to his head like unaccustomed wine.

Rita Bellamy came into the hall to meet him. "How are you feeling?" she asked anxiously.

"A bit shaky since I got on my feet," Ralph answered.

"Come into the lounge and sit down. I'll make some tea. You've time for a cup before you go back to the mill, haven't you, Henry?" she asked her husband as he followed Ralph into the house.

It was a minute or so before her words seemed to register. "No thanks," he said at last. "I don't want one. I'm not going back to the mill today. I'm going upstairs for a rest."

Rita gazed after him anxiously as he left them.

"What's got into Dad?" Ralph asked her.

"He's not well," her voice was preoccupied. "This business of yours was a terrible shock." She left him and went to make the tea. She didn't want to discuss the attack with Ralph. She still found it impossible to believe that Stephen had been responsible, in spite of her stepson's statement. She felt that Ralph, as well as Henry, was becoming more of a puzzle every day.

"You're not thinking of going back to the mill for a few days, I hope," she said to Ralph when she took the tea in.

He looked at her thoughtfully, and then said, "Rita," for she had instructed him to use her Christian name, understanding that he would never be able to bring himself to call her 'mother,' "do you remember telling me to fight for what I wanted?"

"Yes. I said you ought to carry on fighting for Wendy—but I didn't mean in the sense of literal blows. I never expected you to end up in hospital."

"I'm not thinking of Wendy just now," he responded. "I'm thinking of my job at the mill. I hate it!"

She was shattered by the vehemence in his tone.

"I don't want to go back there—ever, but you know how Dad feels. He thinks I'll automatically step into his shoes one day. I won't, you know. They'll never fit!"

"I didn't realize you felt so strongly about it," Rita answered slowly. This was something she hadn't bargained for. She wondered how many other violent likes and dislikes Ralph had kept bottled up all these years underneath his placid exterior.

"What kind of work would you like to do?" she asked him.

"Something connected with children or young people. I'd have liked to have trained as a teacher, but there was no point in mentioning it to Dad. He's always had a one track mind as far as I've been concerned."

"Do you want me to have a word with him?" Rita offered.

"No—thanks all the same," he answered with a new confidence. "I'll tell him myself."

Upstairs Henry sat by the window, passing his hand across his eyes. His head throbbed so unbearably that it was almost impossible to think clearly.

Rita was worried about him, he knew. She hadn't commented upon his strained exhausted look, probably realizing he'd only lose his temper if she did. He hadn't given her much of a life lately. He must make it up to her when all this was over—if ever it would be over for him!

He'd lived in a semi-nightmare ever since the news of Ralph's injury. When the first sharp anxiety about his son had worn off, and the rumors about Stephen had begun to circulate, he had experienced a sense of relief. Now, surely, the minister would be finished.

But the relief had been short lived. Drawn, as men often are, to the scenes associated with their guilt, he had driven out past the Wayside Garage during the week end, after hearing that Bill Jennings had left the town. He had intended suggesting diplomatically to Ernie Briggs that he would be going on a wild goose chase if he tried to track Jennings down. But he'd been too late. When he'd reached the garage, Briggs was already deep in conversation with Sergeant Brown. Having discovered that Jennings had left Redford, he had reported the theft of the materials from the garage, and now the chase was on.

When they caught Jennings, just how many facts would come to light, Henry wondered desperately, remembering that they had parted on bad terms.

The walls of the room seemed to be closing in on him. He got up restlessly. He would go out for a walk. Perhaps the fresh air would clear his head.

He went mechanically down the drive, blind to the beauty of his early roses. Automatically he turned toward the town—his town, the place where he was respected, held up as an example of prosperity resulting from hard work and integrity. Integrity! The word mocked him.

At last he came to Blakelock Hill. Why had he come in this direction? His associations with the old Chapel were over. Yet it seemed, in spite of himself, he continued walking until he came to the shabby, familiar door. It was open, as he had known it would be.

He stepped inside, and the sunshine, filtering through a distant window, fell directly into his eyes. He moved out of the shaft of light, and then realized that he was not alone. Stephen Thornton was kneeling in the front pew.

Henry hesitated. This was a possibility he had not anticipated. He stood still, wondering if he could slip out without attracting the minister's attention. But even as he watched, Stephen raised his head and looked up at the plain wooden cross above the pulpit. The sunlight fell across his face, and Henry could see his expression. Stephen Thornton, in spite of the pressure he was under, was at peace. He knew where to take his problems!

He, too, as a lifelong member of the Chapel, should have been able to find refuge here, Henry reflected. But by his inconsistent actions he had forfeited all claims to the comfort of the Christian faith. There was no way through to communion with Christ. Quietly, with a last glance at Stephen, that had in it for the first time a hint of compassion, Henry moved toward the door, a broken man.

CHAPTER NINETEEN

Roy Wilson reached Moorfield at about ten-thirty on Monday morning. Pulling his motor bike to the curb on one of the quieter streets, he studied the newspaper he had taken from Jennings' lodgings. After several enquiries, he managed to locate the first of the garages underlined in the advertisements columns.

It was a large concern, and two men were busily employed on the gas pumps. Roy waited until one of them was free.

Approaching him, he indicated the newspaper he was carrying. "I've come about this ad," he began. But before he could explain that he was not after the job himself, the attendant replied, "The job's gone, mate. That bloke over there got it."

Roy's second call proved as fruitless. It took him quite a while to locate the third garage. It was on the opposite side of the town in a much poorer quarter, perfect 'Jennings' country' Roy reflected wryly.

It was past lunch time when he parked his bike on the opposite side of the street and walked slowly across to the garage. It was quiet and obviously didn't do much trade. After a few minutes, however, a small van drew up and Jennings came on to the forecourt.

As he moved toward the van, he caught sight of Roy, and his face was a picture of shocked dismay. Roy made no obvious sign of recognition, and remained motionless until the van had been driven away. Then in a few lengthy strides, he reached Jennings.

"How did you find out where I was?" the man blustered. "Why have you followed me here?"

"You left quite a few unfinished deals back in Redford, didn't you?" Roy challenged him. "Ernie Briggs has missed a number of things, and your rent is unpaid, but there are more important issues. That raincoat I saw in your room last Friday night! You left it behind in Redford, didn't you?"

"I don't know what you're talking about," Jennings hedged. "But if you don't let me get on with my work, you'll get me the sack."

"That would be a pleasure," Roy said grimly. "I've only to walk in that office and give your new boss a few details, and you'd be down the road right away."

"You won't, though!" Jennings pleaded.

"Why shouldn't I?"

"Because we were mates."

"Don't make me laugh!" Roy sneered. "I'll keep my mouth shut on one condition."

"What's that?" Jennings asked uneasily.

"That you meet me immediately you've finished work here, and answer a few questions."

"All right. I'll be free at five o'clock," Jennings edged away.

"Don't try anything smart," Roy warned him. "I'll be watching the place."

He stationed himself in a passage opposite the garage and settled down to his vigil. Jennings knew he was cornered. He would have to give Roy the information he was after. Perhaps if he did, the lad would go back to Redford and leave him alone.

When he came off duty, Roy walked over to meet him. "I haven't eaten for hours, and I suppose you could do with a meal," he said to Jennings. "Where's a likely place around here?"

"There's a cafe down this street," was the answer.

He led the way to a dingy looking place and glanced back enquiringly.

They entered, picking their way between the littered tables to a distant corner. When they had been served with greasy fish and chips by a disinterested girl in faded overalls, Roy leaned across the table. "Now," he said, "let's get down to business."

"What do you want from me?" Jennings asked cautiously.

"Information!" Roy answered. "And I'm not going to pay you for it, either. I've got the whip hand now, because I know what happened on Friday night!"

Jennings affected an air of bewildered innocence, but Roy continued, "I want to know what you had on Henry Bellamy. Why

114

did he come to talk to you at the garage that time? What was he paying you for?"

"It can't be of any interest to you," Jennings objected.

"It's of interest to my father. He feels that Bellamy owes him something," Roy answered.

At last Jennings capitulated. After all, he reflected, he could never go back to Redford again, and it looked as if he'd got all he was ever likely to get out of Henry Bellamy.

"What I have on Bellamy is enough to finish him in Redford," he said maliciously. "You see," he paused dramatically, "he stole the money from the mill—not John Thornton!"

"How do you know?" Roy asked.

"I saw the whole thing," Jennings told him. "I was employed at the Albion Mill at the time on maintenance work. I was doing some repairs to the roof of the weaving shed. It was directly opposite and level with the windows of Henry Bellamy's office. He was cashier at the time. His wife had been ill—she was never very fit, and she died not long after all this happened.

"The work I was doing that day was hard," Jennings continued, "and every now and then I stopped for a breather. During one of these, I glanced across into the office, and saw Bellamy go to the safe. There was nothing unusual in that, for he had access to it in the course of his job. But it was the stealthy way he went about opening it and taking out some money that attracted my curiosity. He kept looking over his shoulder, as though afraid in case anyone should come in and catch him. Then he transferred a bundle of notes to his briefcase. I was fascinated by what I'd seen, and I spent the rest of the morning watching him."

"Not long afterwards two men came to the Mill. I'd seen them around before, knew they were the auditors. They went up to Bellamy's office. It was obvious that he hadn't been expecting them, and it wasn't one of their routine visits. You should have seen his face! They settled down at his desk and got to work on the books, and there was Bellamy, his briefcase stuffed with the firm's money, unable to put it back because they'd planted themselves between him and the safe!"

"What did he do?" Roy asked, already guessing the answer.

"He panicked, realizing, I suppose, that it was only a matter of time before the theft was discovered. He picked up the briefcase under his jacket, and slipped out of the room while they were working. John Thornton was assistant cashier in those days, and his office was next to Bellamy's. Bellamy went into his office, which was empty, took the bundle of notes out of his briefcase, and put it into the pocket of an overcoat hanging in the corner."

"John Thornton's coat!" Roy surmised.

"Yes. The remainder of the story I heard later from a man who worked in the office," Jennings concluded. "It seems there had been some fiddling going on for a time, and the auditors had been sent for without the staff being notified. There was naturally a discrepancy between the figures in the books and the cash in the safe; Bellamy hadn't had time to make any adjustments. John Thornton had access to the safe. He was known to be in debt and of an unstable character. When the hue and cry was raised and the money discovered in his coat pocket, no one really questioned it."

"But you could have cleared him," Roy said. "Why didn't you?"

"And lose the chance of an assured income?" Jennings grinned sardonically.

"You made up your mind right at the beginning that you'd blackmail Henry Bellamy," Roy said in disgust. "And you've been living on him ever since."

"On and off. You don't need to look down your nose at me, either," Jennings finished. "You're no better. You only wanted this information to pass on to your father so that he can work on Bellamy!" He pushed back his chair. "Well—you've got what you came for. I'm going now, and you needn't follow me. We made a bargain—remember."

Roy didn't answer. He felt soiled, cheapened by the encounter, and the scornful words with which the fellow had condemned him echoed in his mind, "You're no better!"

He wasn't, Roy reflected, the beginnings of self-disgust gnawing at him. He felt ashamed of himself as he got to his feet, paid the bill and went out.

CHAPTER TWENTY

When Stephen Thornton returned to his lodgings from the Chapel that afternoon, he saw that he had a visitor. The car standing outside the front gate was the familiar one in which he had traveled to Redford that March day. He remembered the letter he had posted to Andrew Gardener on Saturday. He hadn't expected such swift action.

"Mr. Gardener just arrived, Mr. Thornton," Anne Ogden told him as he entered the house.

Bracing himself, Stephen opened the door of his room.

Andrew Gardener looked up and greeted him calmly. Not by the slightest change of expression did he betray how shocked he was by the minister's appearance.

"Let's have some tea before we talk, Stephen," he said, taking the initiative.

"I didn't expect you so soon," Stephen told him.

"I set off immediately after I received your letter," the older man replied. "The situation sounded rather desperate."

"It is," Stephen admitted, adding sincerely, "I'm glad to have you here." It was a welcome relief to have someone more experienced to turn to.

His companion did not refer again to the contents of his letter until they had finished their tea, then he said simply, "You'd better tell me the whole story."

Stephen omitted nothing. He stated that he and Wendy Craig had been childhood sweethearts in the days before his family had left Redford, and that when her engagement to Ralph Bellamy had been broken off, he had, without realizing it, been blamed. He told of the mistakenly accepted lift in her car, resulting in the crash,

117

and finished with the account of the attack on Ralph, explaining the facts he had given to Donald Waring, and the doctor's theory.

"It's this not knowing what really happened that's so worrying," he said. "It's dreadful to think I may have been responsible for Ralph's injuries."

Andrew Gardener studied him closely. "And the police?" he questioned. "You stated they'd suspected you because they'd found your raincoat nearby. Have there been any further developments?"

Stephen shook his head. "They've left me alone since Saturday," he replied. "I told them my raincoat was missing before the night in question, but I must have sounded terribly vague. Everything's been so confusing since the accident."

Andrew Gardener leaned back. "Well, I don't think there's much we can do tonight," he said. "Tomorrow I'll see the various people involved. And I'll have to call a special members' meeting." He paused, "I shall ask all those who have resigned because of these recent developments to come," he finished.

"And you'll thrash the whole thing out and ask for a vote of confidence?" Stephen assumed.

"Yes," the older man studied his downcast face in concern. "It's the only course open to me, Stephen. I believe in you, implicitly, but for the sake of the work here, it's essential that these people should believe in you, too. The cause is more important than the individual. We cannot allow that to be harmed, whatever the personal cost involved. I warned you this was stony ground," he finished gently. "Now you've found out for yourself just how rough it is. At the moment this may seem like the end of everything. But you're young—there are other places of service."

"Redford was a challenge!" Stephen looked up, his eyes dark with feeling. "I refuse to believe I've lost it—yet."

Andrew Gardener smiled, relieved to see that he still had some fighting spirit left. "You may not have lost it," he said encouragingly. "I said there wasn't much we could do tonight, but there is! We can talk to the Lord about it together."

They knelt down at opposite sides of the hearth; the old minister with the memory of God's deliverance from many difficult situations to inspire him, and the young man with nothing but faith to go on.

When Andrew Gardener had placed the complex problem in

118

God's hands, and Stephen had added his own halting prayer, they rose feeling calmer and stronger.

The older man glanced at his watch. He was looking tired. "If you don't mind, Stephen, I'll turn in early," he said. "Mrs. Ogden kindly prepared the spare room as soon as I arrived. It's been a long day."

"Yes, of course. You get some rest," Stephen replied.

Later he opened the front door and walked down the narrow flagged path to the gate. It was a beautiful night, the sun setting above the distant hills, their uneven peaks darkly silhouetted against the reddish gold sky; the white and yellow roses in the front garden giving off their fragrance in the tranquil air.

Stephen stood letting the peaceful loveliness of the scene soak into his battered spirit, reminding himself that the God who had created all this beauty was well able to take care of him.

Then he heard footsteps approaching, and Jean Collins turned the corner of the road. She started slightly as he spoke to her, for he was partly screened from view by the trees between the two gardens.

"I'm sorry if I gave you a shock," he apologized.

"It's all right," she smiled. "I'm glad I've seen you, Mr. Thornton. We were talking at the Wilsons' yesterday about the— attack on Ralph Bellamy," she went on diffidently. "I remembered that you weren't wearing your raincoat for a week or more before Ralph was hurt. You remember—the night after Wendy's accident —we walked up High Street and I remarked about the fact that you were unprepared for the storm? You said then you'd mislaid your raincoat."

"Yes," Stephen took his mind back over the troubled, confused days.

"Well—I thought I ought to tell the police," Jean went on. "I hoped it would help if someone else confirmed the fact that the coat had been missing. So I went to the station and made a statement."

"Thank you," he said simply. He was deeply touched. All the more so when he recollected Jean as she had been in those early days in Redford, engrossed in herself and cynical and bitter. She had changed so much. He was glad she believed in him. Somehow the way ahead no longer seemed quite so desolate.

"It was the least I could do," she answered, turning to walk up

119

the path to the adjoining house. "Goodnight, Mr. Thornton. I hope everything works out all right."

"Goodnight, Jean!" He was not aware that he had used her Christian name for the first time, as he stood watching her walk away.

In the hall Jean hung up her light summer coat. She had been surprised by his unexpected use of her Christian name, and her thoughts whirled in a strange new confusion. When Roy opened the living room door and called to her, she realized she didn't want to join the family.

"I'm tired tonight, Roy," she told him, going on up to her room.

"All right," he said, closing the door and turning back to his father and Jennifer. His mother was out visiting a sick neighbor. For once Roy was glad that Jean didn't want to join them. He wasn't anxious for her to know about his activities that day.

"Come on! Tell us all about it!" Jennifer demanded. "You've been hinting ever since you came in that you'd some startling news."

Roy, aware that for once he had his father's full attention, told of his visit to Jennings' lodgings on Friday night, and his subsequent call on Sunday afternoon.

Jim Wilson listened in mounting satisfaction as Roy told how he had traced Jennings and badgered the truth out of him. At last he was in a position to settle the old account with Henry Bellamy!

"Not a word about this to anyone else," he instructed his son and daughter. "And don't say anything to your mother. She'd insist on coming out with the truth, if only for young Thornton's sake."

Roy was silent, experiencing again that nagging sense of guilt which had haunted him ever since he had parted from Jennings. If he kept the truth to himself, could he go on behaving normally knowing that it was in his power to put right an old wrong, and to save a young man's career?

120

CHAPTER TWENTY-ONE

The following day the Rev. Andrew Gardener called on the various members, and succeeded in organizing a meeting to take place that same evening.

He realized how bad the situation looked for the young minister. Practically everywhere he had met with the same reaction. Inspite of the initial welcome the people had given Stephen, they had been predisposed to anticipate failure on his part because he was John Thornton's son. No one else would have had it quite so tough, Andrew realized, but then no one else had been so eager to take on such a difficult place.

At last it was time for the meeting to begin. Stephen, looking pale and strained, followed Mr. Gardener on to the platform. The three members of the Bellamy family, Henry staring stonily in front of him, were at one side of the Chapel. Hubert Craig and his wife, who looked ill and nervous, were seated at the other side. A little further along on the same row, with several empty places between, Jean Collins was sitting with Jennifer Wilson and her mother, and, Stephen noticed in surprise, Roy was with them for the first time. Catherine Williams sat in the middle of a row near the front, and as her eyes met Stephen's, she gave him an encouraging smile. Donald Waring, coming in late, sat near the back.

Andrew Gardener announced the opening hymn, the familiar and well-loved "Onward, Christian Soldiers."

"I have chosen this hymn purposely to remind you that we are, above all, Christ's soldiers," he began, "commissioned to go out and extend His Kingdom. Nothing must be allowed to hinder our calling. Satan has successfully managed to split up the ranks in this

121

place. We must remember that an army divided within itself isn't likely to be victorious."

His words set the tone of the meeting, bringing home to the people the importance of the issues at stake. Those who had attended from a desire to hear something sensational, began to be ashamed of their motives. There was a very real sense of the presence of God.

During the second verse of the hymn, Eleanor Craig whispered to her husband that she didn't feel very well. But Hubert's expression was unusually firm as he answered, "We're both staying to see this through. Don't forget how deeply Wendy has been involved."

Rita Bellamy glanced up at her husband. He was standing motionless, not attempting to sing. Ralph gazed fixedly at some point in the far distance. He seemed to be unable to look directly at Stephen Thornton.

When the congregation sat down again, Mr. Gardener began, "I understand there have been certain allegations made against your pastor resulting in a state of disruption in the work here. As far as I have been able to ascertain, there is no proof that there is any truth in these allegations. But this isn't a court of law, and we are not here to sit in judgment on anyone. What we are here for is to try to find a satisfactory solution to our differences, so that the work may go on. Before we come to a discussion of our problems, however, I think we ought to have a time of prayer, so that we can allow God to search our hearts and examine our motives, to make sure there is nothing in us likely to hinder His work. We shall do this immediately after Mr. Thornton has said a few words."

Stephen got to his feet, aware of the cold wave of hostility that swept through the gathering.

"I came back to Redford to work among you," he began hesitatingly, "because I have always cherished a deep love for this place and its people, inspite of the painful memories associated with it."

Roy Wilson glanced uncomfortably down at his shoes. Undoubtedly the minister was referring to that business about his father.

"Many of you knew and loved my grandfather," Stephen continued. "Probably a number of you came to know Christ during the revival under his ministry. When I came here I hoped and prayed for a similar revival—not with the idea of proving I'm as good a minister as he was. I don't think I ever will be. But I felt, and still feel, that revival is the only answer to the problems of our times. But where men work and pray for revival, Satan is at his busiest, for he will not suffer an intrusion into his kingdom lightly. I believe that he has used the recent unfortunate set of incidents, not solely to discredit me—I'm not of such importance, but rather to put a stumbling block in the way of God's blessing on this town. I want you to think about that as we pray. For myself—whatever the future holds—I shall always pray for a revival in this place, whether I am here to take an active part in it or not. God is my judge that in so far as I consciously know, I have done nothing to bring discredit upon His cause, and I am content to wait for Him to vindicate me in His own time and way, and to reveal the truth that shall ultimately make us all free from this cloud."

There was a silence that could almost be felt as he sat down, and many of the people present were unable to meet his eyes.

Then Mr. Gardener took control of the meeting, and when he led the congregation in prayer his voice was diffident, almost as if he were half afraid of disturbing that tangible sense of God's presence.

Then—after a long pause, into the trembling silence came the broken, halting tones of a desperate man.

"The truth shall make you free!" Henry Bellamy's voice wavered over the words, as he got to his feet and gripped the edge of the pew in front of him. "Perhaps no one has any right to understand the truth of those words better than I have." He stopped, then stumbled on shakily, "God forgive me, but for the past eight years, I have been a living lie!"

The shocked people raised their heads, but he was not aware of their startled glances. He wasn't even conscious of Rita's hand in sudden sympathy upon his clenched one, or of Ralph's shattered expression. His gaze was fixed on the plain wooden cross above the pulpit.

"You have all been ready to believe the worst of Mr. Thornton, because of his father's reputation. But I have to confess to you that his father was innocent of the charge of theft. I took the firm's money and when I realized my action was bound to be discovered, I panicked, and fixed the evidence so that John Thornton was blamed."

Roy Wilson's head went down on his hands, as with a great sense of release he saw that he need contribute no further to the monstrous web of lies. He was free from his sordid deal with Jennings—free to begin life on a new level!

Stephen looked up dazedly as the mill manager went on, "I've lived in a private hell of my own ever since. Mr. Thornton's return here raked up the whole business again in my conscience until I couldn't bear it. That was why I opposed him in everything. I know I deserve nothing but censure from all of you. I'm so sorry—so terribly sorry," he turned and almost stumbled over his son's feet as he groped his way blindly towards the aisle, and staggered out of the building.

A few yards away Ethel Blake was staring blankly in front of her, her face a stony mask of bewilderment as her lifelong idol crashed at her feet. But Rita Bellamy, with a new tenderness in her face, rose quietly and went after her husband. And in the silence which followed Ralph stood up. This was one time when he knew he had to follow in his father's footsteps.

Aware of the curious glances of the young people who had looked up to him, he began, "I, too, have the need to say I'm sorry, to Mr. Thornton and to all of you. That statement I made about how I got hurt last Friday night wasn't true. I never had any argument with Mr. Thornton. I saw him hurrying after me, and because I didn't want to talk to him, I turned down a side street. After a minute or so I looked back and saw him pass the end of it. He had evidently lost track of me. It was quite a while after this that I got knocked out. I never saw who did it."

He was conscious of the astonished gasps that came from the listening people, and continued with an effort, "By the lunch time mail today, I received a note from Wendy Craig, enclosing a statement which she asked me to pass on to you. Perhaps you would read it, Mr. Gardener." He walked up the aisle and passed the folded sheet of paper to the minister.

Andrew Gardener smoothed it out. Stephen seemed too bewildered by this unexpected turn of events to take in all that was happening.

Then Mr. Gardener read what Wendy had written. "I've been told while in the hospital of all the unpleasantness caused to Mr. Thornton by some quite unnecessary speculation as to the circumstances and cause of the accident in which we were both involved," she had said. "I wish to make it quite clear that Mr. Thornton was in no way to blame for it, nor was there any need for gossip. Since his return to Redford we have been nothing more than friends. The accident happened because I was talking, and took my attention off the road. Mr. Thornton, who had accepted my offer of a lift because the weather looked stormy, immediately tried to right the car when I lost control of it. When he saw the crash was inevitable, he tried to protect me from the worst of the impact."

The minister put down the letter and said quietly, "It seems that the Spirit of God has been at work here before this meeting began. Three people, without human prompting, have confessed the truth and clarified the situation. It may be that Mr. Thornton's prayers for revival are nearer to being answered than he has dared to believe. Perhaps there are others present who feel the need to get right with God. It may be that your guilt does not personally affect other people here tonight. Unlike these other cases, there may be nothing gained by a public confession. But God knows our hearts, and the important issue is that we are reconciled to Him. He is willing to forgive all our sins and mistakes, if only we will turn to Him in sincere repentance."

Other prayers followed. More than one person asked forgiveness for being so ready to pass on gossip. Jean Collins, her heart full of wonder at this unexpected revelation of divine power at work, became slowly aware of the stifled sobbing of the woman sitting further along the row. Earlier she had regretted the fact that in her hurry to find a seat she had chosen the same pew as Eleanor Craig! Now she knew why she had been guided to it. Like everything else that was happening tonight, it had been ordained by God.

Prompted by the compassion that had become an essential part of her new nature, Jean laid a comforting hand on the shoulder of the woman she had come to Redford to find.

Eleanor lifted a startled face. "Jean!" she whispered, then seeing the girl's expression she added brokenly, "You know who I am now—don't you?"

Jean nodded. "I've known for a few days, but don't upset yourself. It doesn't matter any more." And she realized it didn't. The love of God had filled her heart, obliterating all grievances. She had come here seeking revenge, but God had met with her and given her love and hope, and all she wanted now was that others should share in her joy.

And so the meeting went on. The summer darkness fell, someone switched on the lights, and the hands on the clock above the

125

main door moved unnoticed. Time had become unimportant. Everything was forgotten except the compelling need to get right with God.

The lights in the Chapel shone far into the night, and in another lighted building, the Police Station, the missing pieces in the jigsaw pattern of events were being supplied, as Bill Jennings was brought to account at last.

The police, following Ernie Briggs report of the thefts from the garage, and observing Roy's efforts to trace Jennings, had followed Roy to Moorfield, and finally caught up with Jennings when he and Roy had parted company. Knowing that the game was up, Jennings had confessed that following a quarrel with Henry Bellamy, he had gone out, and knowing something of Ralph's recently acquired habit of walking the town at night, had followed him, knocked him out and stolen his wallet. Then, to throw the police off the scent, he had left the minister's raincoat nearby—the raincoat he had stolen from Wendy Craig's car after it had been towed into the garage following the crash.

When the Chapel door had closed behind her, Rita Bellamy hesitated, wondering which way Henry had gone. Intuition told her he would not go straight back to Hillcrest, and the car was still parked near the Chapel. She stepped out into the summer dusk and walked down the hill into the town. Fearful of what Henry might do in his present state of mind, she hurried along High Street. Then, glancing up at the mill, she saw that a light was on in the gloomy old building—his office light.

Almost running, she rounded the corner of the street which gave access to the mill, flung herself through the main door and hurried up the steep flight of stairs. Henry was slumped at his desk an empty bottle in front of him, some tablets in his hand, a glass of water by his elbow.

She raced across the room, knocking the tablets to the floor.

"Rita!" He raised an ashen face.

"What do you think you're doing?" she demanded.

"I'm finished. Don't you understand? Finished!" His face crumpled, his distraught glance swept the room. "Finished here and in the town."

"And so you decided to take the coward's way out just when I was coming to tell you how proud of you I am," she turned on him.

"Proud of me—a thief and a liar!" he echoed unbelievingly.

126

"Proud of you for being man enough to try to put things right even at this late stage," she said in a gentler voice. "All these years there has been a barrier between us. Now it's gone. What does it matter if you are finished here? The mill doesn't own your soul. You'll be able to live with yourself again. We still have our life together. I'll stand by you."

He looked up and understood for the first time the real woman she was beneath the sophisticated exterior she had turned to the world to mask her own unhappiness.

"I want to tell you how it happened," he said in a low voice. "Ralph's mother was an invalid. It made her—demanding. Because I was so sorry for her, I couldn't deny her the luxuries she craved for, even when I couldn't afford them, and had to resort to dishonest means to provide them. At last I was in debt to such an extent I had to do something desperate."

"It doesn't matter any more," Rita told him. "Most of the people involved are gone—Ralph's mother and John Thornton and his wife. But you've set Stephen free from the stigma. You've done all that's humanly possible, Henry. You must accept God's forgiveness and learn to forgive yourself."

"Do you think I'll ever be able to do that—ever hold up my head again in Redford?" he asked her.

"Yes—in time. You won't be the only one having to make adjustments, either. Something tells me there are going to be many changes in Redford—and it'll be a good thing! Come along home, Henry. God willing we still have some years in which to make restitution."

Slowly he got to his feet, took a last look around his office, and then followed her out into the night without another backward glance.

127

CHAPTER TWENTY-TWO

On the Thursday morning following that memorable service, Stephen was sitting alone in his room planning the meetings for the weekend.

He hadn't noticed that the doorbell had rung, but Anne Ogden looked in to say that Mrs. Craig wanted to see him.

Eleanor looked pale and tired but there was a new composure about her.

"Come and sit down, Mrs. Craig," Stephen invited, drawing up a chair.

She complied willingly. "I had to come to see you, Stephen— Mr. Thornton, to tell you how sorry I am for all the things I said about you the night of Wendy's accident. I was so upset about everything. She seemed to be making such a mess of her life when it had all been planned so carefully. That was the trouble. I was too ambitious for Wendy. But I wanted her to have all the things I never had. Perhaps you'll understand when I've told you my story."

"You don't have to tell me anything, Mrs. Craig," he pointed out. "You can talk it over with the Lord."

"Believe me I've already done that! But I want you to have all the facts because—I need your help."

"Very well."

"I had a vastly different start in life than Wendy," she began. "There were two of us at home, my sister, Jean, and I. My mother was a widow and an invalid. It was a hard life for two young girls. I made up my mind that I'd get away from it at the first opportunity. Jean's attitude was totally different. She was the patient, uncomplaining type. I made up my mind to marry a man with money and social prestige. I wasn't ever going to struggle on a low income as my mother had been compelled to do. Jean used to say, however, that she would marry only for love."

"When my mother died we sold up the home and went our separate ways. I drifted from one job to another, moving from town to town, always trying to improve my circumstances. I ended up in Redford during the war, and worked in a munitions factory. I lost touch with Jean. Hubert and I met, and were mutually attracted. He'd had everything in life that I'd been denied. Things seemed to be working out very well. Hubert wasn't conscripted into the Forces because he had some slight heart condition, and he remained here managing the family business."

"Then, just as everything I'd worked for seemed within my grasp, I heard an S.O.S. message on the radio. My sister was dangerously ill in a hospital in the midlands. Neither Hubert nor any of my close friends in Redford heard the message, and I left without telling them the reason. When I reached the hospital Jean had died. It was then I learned that she'd been married to a young man serving in the Navy. He'd been killed in action not long afterwards. There was a baby, a little girl, then being cared for by Jean's landlady. I went to see the woman—a Mrs. Collins," Eleanor continued with difficulty. She saw Stephen start at the mention of the familiar name, and forced herself to go on.

"The baby was called Jean, too, and was the image of her mother. I stayed in that poor little room until Jean's funeral was over, and all the time I wondered about that baby. I was her only living relative. I knew I ought to take care of her, but I was completely selfish. I'd given Hubert a picture of my own background, telling him all my relatives had died years before, making him believe I'd come from a wealthy home. I wasn't sure of him and I believed it would ruin my chances altogether if I returned to Redford with a baby belonging to a sister I'd never admitted having! I told Mrs. Collins I'd have to go back to my lodgings, and make arrangements about taking the baby there at a later date, and asked her to carry on looking after little Jean until I'd fixed things up. But—" her voice trailed off uncomfortably.

"You never went back for the child," Stephen finished grimly.

"No. I tried to tell myself that I was justified in my action. Mrs. Collins was completely devoted to the baby. She'd lost her own little girl in an air raid, and she'd looked after Jean almost from birth for my sister had been ill most of the time. I told myself that

Jean would be better off with a woman who really needed her, rather than with a relative who'd regard her as something of a handicap."

"I suppose you've got something there," Stephen commented. "But didn't Mrs. Collins ever try to find you?"

"I hadn't made it very easy for her," Mrs. Craig answered. "I never told her which town I'd come from in answer to the S.O.S. message, and I think she was too shocked and confused by everything to remember my surname. She just knew me as Nell, short for Ellen. I called myself Eleanor to impress Hubert and his family."

"But from what I know of Mr. Craig, he wouldn't have walked out on you if you'd decided to adopt an orphaned niece," Stephen remarked.

"I know that now! I've known it for a long time," she answered. "But I wasn't sure of it or of him then. He was so terribly swayed by his family, and they were suspicious of every girl friend he'd ever had. And afterwards, when I realized Hubert wouldn't have minded, it was too late. He'd have despised me for lying to him. At least," she qualified, "that's what I thought until the meeting on Tuesday night. And then I knew I'd have to tell him, whatever the consequences. I've never had a minute's peace of mind since Jean Collins turned up in Redford."

"It was strange how she found me," Eleanor explained. "She told me all about it after the service the other night. She grew up believing that Mrs. Collins was her real mother, for although the woman never adopted her legally, she called her by her own name, letting her take the place of the child she had lost. It wasn't until after Mrs. Collins' death, when Jean was going through some private papers, that she stumbled on the true facts through finding her birth certificate. That started her making enquiries. And an old neighbor told her what she knew of the story. Among some letters Jean found a note from a friend of Mrs. Collins. This woman, traveling north, had picked up a copy of the *Redford Gazette* and seen the photograph of a group of us outside the factory. She recognized me, having met me at Jean's funeral. I suppose she thought Mrs. Collins would be anxious to trace me. But she never took any action, proof that she didn't want to part with Jean."

"And Jean made up her mind to track you down," Stephen said.

"Yes. I was afraid she might be successful, and that Hubert and Wendy would learn what I'd done. So—I sent her threatening letters. Of course I wouldn't have done her any harm. I just wanted to frighten her away from Redford."

"And now the truth has come out," he replied quietly, "it has made you free!"

"Yes—and it's a wonderful feeling. I told Hubert the whole story on Tuesday night. He was very understanding. But then, he always has been. He insisted that we owed it to Jean to make up to her all that she should have had from us over the years. After we'd told Wendy, Hubert went to see Jean, to offer her a home with us. But she refused it. Not because she bears any malice, but because she feels she would rather carry on in the kind of home and way of life she's been used to. That's where I need your help, Stephen," she finished, "I want you to persuade her to come to us."

"But what about Wendy?" he pointed out. "How does she feel about sharing her home with a newly acquired cousin?"

"Wendy's changed. She won't mind," Eleanor answered. "You know what she's thinking of doing?"

He shook his head, remembering how unpredictable Wendy was.

"She wants to take up nursing. I don't suppose it will amount to anything, after the easy life she's been used to."

"You won't try to stop her?" Stephen pleaded.

"No," she replied. "I've finished trying to re-live my life through her." She got to her feet. "Thanks for listening, Mr. Thornton. You'll talk to Jean, won't you?"

"I'll do my best," he promised. "But don't be surprised if I'm not successful. Jean Collins has a very definite mind of her own!"

He went to the door with her, and as he was returning to his own room, William Ogden came into the hall, and handed him the new issue of the *Redford Gazette*.

"There's an account of Tuesday night's meeting in it, Mr. Thornton," he told the minister.

Stephen took the newspaper back to his room. Catherine Williams had done a good job, he reflected. He must ring her up and thank her.

When he eventually got through to her from the call box, and told her of his gratitude, she said casually, "It's all in a day's work."

"I shall always be thankful for what you've done," he told her.

"No. You must forget the past. You're the man who's only

132

interested in the future," she reminded him. "And there's a great future for you in Redford. The other churches in the district will be eager to work for the campaign now they've seen some practical results at Blakelock Hill. There'll be some good write-ups from us. I've got Mr. Ellis really interested, so even after I've left," she stopped abruptly.

Stephen fastened on the remark. "You're not leaving Redford?"

"Yes," her voice sounded flat. "I've got the chance of a job on one of the city newspapers. I'd be a fool not to take it."

"Well—you must think about your future," he replied quietly. "But we shall miss you."

"There'll be someone else to take up where I leave off. I think young Jennifer Wilson is coming to work for the *Gazette*. She's fed up with her job at the mill. Well, I must go. I'm still on the payroll here, and I've spent long enough talking. 'Bye, Stephen!"

He felt the forced heartiness in her tone, and replaced the receiver with a frown. He had the uncanny feeling that it wasn't ambition alone that was forcing Catherine to leave Redford.

He passed a remark about their telephone conversation to Donald Waring when, later in the day, he encountered the doctor coming out of the Post Office.

"Catherine leaving!" Donald echoed blankly. "Why, I thought that was the last thing she'd do."

"Hasn't she mentioned it to you?" Stephen queried in surprise.

"Why should she?" Donald countered. "I'm sorry about this, Stephen. It must be a blow—just when everything seemed to be straightening out."

"Well—yes. I shall miss her at the Chapel," the minister answered.

"You're taking it very calmly!" Donald exclaimed.

"Catherine has her future to think of," was the reply.

"But," Donald turned to him, "I thought her future was tied up with yours!"

It was Stephen's turn to look astounded. "You thought Catherine and I—" he broke off. "You're way off beam, Donald."

"But—she's been so quick to defend you. I thought that when all this gossip died down you'd be making plans together."

"No," Stephen assured him. "Catherine just went all out to see justice done to the work of God. If you're looking for the person she's attracted to, you'd better look nearer home!" he finished meaningly.

His words stayed with Donald for the rest of the morning. At lunch time he went to the cafe on High Street where Catherine often had her meals. She was there—alone. He walked purposefully over to her.

"Donald!" She turned and started. "I wasn't expecting you."

"I came to talk to you," he said directly. "Why are you leaving Redford, Catherine?"

"I want to see a bit of the world. Besides, my job here is finished now."

"Now that things have cleared up for Stephen?"

"Yes. I felt I had to see that through."

"I don't suppose it's entered your head that someone else in Redford may need you?" he questioned bluntly.

She looked away. "No one else made it very apparent," she pointed out.

"That isn't because I didn't want to, Catherine," he replied. "I thought you were in love with Stephen, and I didn't want to spoil things for the two of you."

"And now?" she questioned, looking at him.

"Stephen told me you were leaving, and that there'd been nothing between you, so I came here to tell you," he broke off as he saw her glance past him. The waitress was standing behind him, a very interested expression on her face. He gave their order and turned back to Catherine with a wry grimace. "This is no setting in which to tell you how much I care for you."

"No, it isn't," she smiled. "And I'm really quite romantic at heart. I'd like you to tell me in the old fashioned way, with moonlight and roses and all the rest of it."

"Very well, I will," he promised. "We'll go for a drive tonight. But what about these arrangements you've made to leave Redford? Can you back out of them?"

"Oh, yes," she assured him happily. "They were only plan 'B', made because I never dared believe plan 'A' would materialize. Now it seems as though it's going to work out, I can quite easily scrap plan 'B'."

"Then go ahead and scrap it," he told her, reaching for her hand across the table. "Here's to plan 'A'."

That same afternoon Ralph Bellamy entered the ward in Redford Hospital where Wendy Craig was lying.

She looked surprised to see him, and for a moment there was an awkward silence. Then she said quietly, "Thanks for passing on that letter, and clearing everything up at the meeting on Tuesday night, Ralph. Mum and Dad told me how it went. I've been doing a lot of thinking. I've been a very poor advertisement for Christianity—just used the Chapel for my own ends. But things are going to be different now. I've made a real new start, giving God His rightful place in my life."

"It seems we've both been thinking along the same lines," Ralph answered seriously. "I thought I was following Christ because I was engaged in Christian service. But I wasn't sincere."

"Well now, Stephen looks like he's getting the revival he's worked and prayed for," Wendy answered. "I mean to be a part of it, too, even if I can't be a very active member just yet."

"How much longer are they keeping you in here?" Ralph asked her.

"I'll be going home soon. They're so short of beds," she told him. "It's been an eye-opener to me, Ralph, to see how much sickness and suffering there is. When I'm fit again, I'm thinking of taking up nursing. But now—what about you? Have you got over the attack Jennings made on you?"

"Yes," he smiled. "I think he knocked some sense into my head! I'm not going back to the mill, Wendy."

She stared at him incredulously. "Have you told your father?"

"Oh, yes," his voice was casual. "Of course he's fully occupied with his own affairs at the moment, so it hasn't hit him as hard as it might have done. He's resigning from the mill, you know. I suppose you've heard all about his confession on Tuesday night?"

She nodded her head. "It must have taken some doing. I suppose—his future's pretty uncertain."

Ralph smiled. "Well—Rita's taken him in hand. She's been so good about this. They're talking of selling Hillcrest and buying a small business somewhere in the locality. He was all for leaving, but Rita said that would be a mistake; the talk will die down eventually, and most people will admire him for coming clean at last and having the courage to build up his life all over again. And I think deep in his own heart he wants to stay around to see how things work out at Blakelock Hill. I know he intends compensating Stephen Thornton in any way he can for the harm he's done."

"I'm glad to hear that," Wendy rejoined. "Between us we've given Stephen quite a time of it. And what about you? If you're not going back to the mill, what plans have you made?" she asked him.

"I'm going to train to be a teacher. It's what I've always wanted. I may even follow it up with missionary training, and then offer my services overseas."

She was looking at him with a new respect. He no longer needed to lean on anyone. He knew where he was going, and what he wanted to do with his life.

As though he read her thoughts, he said quietly, "I still love you, Wendy. I always shall. But I must make something of my life before I offer it to you again. Perhaps—in time—we'll come together again—if it's God's will."

She looked away, her eyes suddenly moist. "Yes, Ralph," she answered. "I've a feeling we shall."

When the Chapel members gathered for the communion service on the following Sunday morning, Stephen was aware of the new, deep meaning in their act of worship.

He was glad to see Henry Bellamy taking part; thankful, too, that the other members were treating him normally, and there was no attempt to ostracize him. On Sunday evening the Chapel was almost full, and when at the close of his gospel message Stephen made an appeal, several people responded. Among them he was overjoyed to see Art Wilkins and a member of his gang. He knew he would never have got through to them, had he not passed through these recent difficult experiences.

After the service, Stephen felt the need to be alone. He walked out to the woods on the far side of the town, along the path he had taken on his first Sunday in Redford.

In the calm summer evening the great trees were still, like the massive columns of a living cathedral; the birds' evening hymn muted, stray shafts of sunlight falling through the leafy arches. Conscious of God's majesty, Stephen walked slowly, almost reverently.

Some time elapsed before he realized that he was not alone. A tall slender figure walked ahead of him, the dying sunlight caressing her dark head and lilac-colored dress. Jean Collins! He quickened his steps.

A twig snapped under his foot, and she swung around to face him.

"Stephen!" she exclaimed, then colored in confusion. "I didn't expect to see you out here."

"Nor I you," he smiled. "I've been wanting a talk with you for a few days."

136

She looked up questioningly, and he went on to tell her of her Aunt Eleanor's visit. "She told me how kind you were to her on Tuesday night," he finished. "I'm glad you felt able to forgive her, Jean."

"Well—you were right in what you said that day in the park. She's paid a hundred-fold in mental suffering for what she did. Besides, there's no reason why I should feel sorry for myself. Mrs. Collins was as kind to me as any real mother could have been. God has been very good to me. Step by step He's led me to Himself, and now I can see how He was planning for me all the time when I thought I was alone."

"And you won't need to feel alone any more," he reminded her. "For now you've gained a family. Mrs. Craig told me that she wanted you to make your home with them."

"I suppose she also told you that I'd refused, and asked you to get me to change my mind," Jean commented wryly.

He laughed. "Am I so transparent? But—seriously, why don't you take advantage of her offer? It would give her so much pleasure."

"I feel that I'd be like a fish out of water in that setting," she returned. "I was brought up in a home like the Wilsons'. That's why I've been so comfortable there. But I don't want to hurt Aunt Eleanor's feelings, so I'll probably stay with her from time to time."

"You've no intention of leaving Redford then?" he questioned anxiously.

"No. I've grown quite fond of it. And I want to be a part of the wonderful times ahead for Blakelock Hill Chapel."

"I'm glad to hear you say that," he told her with quiet sincerity. "This place wouldn't be the same without you. I'll never forget that you believed in me when things were at their blackest."

She smiled, "I felt like saying, 'I told you so' to Sergeant Brown, when I heard that Jennings had confessed to the attack on Ralph. I can't imagine how they could have thought you'd done it."

"Well, judging from a conversation I've had with them since, I don't think they really did," Stephen replied. "But they had to have an explanation for my raincoat being found there, and because of that black-out I'd had, my account of my movements was so vague."

She glanced at him compassionately. "It's been a dreadful experience for you," she said, "I'm so glad it's all over."

"So am I, Jean!" The words he had been longing to say to her during the past weeks, but had kept back because of the cloud under which he had been living, came readily now to Stephen's lips. "I can tell you now how much I've come to love you." He looked down at her and saw in the expression in her eyes that his love was returned. "I think I fell in love with you that very first Sunday when I met you out here, and you looked so unhappy," he told her gently.

"It began for me then, Stephen," she answered in a low voice. "Only I fought against it because I was afraid of the challenge of all you believed in."

He took her in his arms, and looking up at him she said, "This is the very place where we parted that Sunday."

"Yes, I remember," he responded. "But this time we won't have to walk separate ways. Through all the future we can walk together in God's service."